DUAL LIVES

DUAL LIVES

GOURAB MITRA

PARTRIDGE
A Penguin Random House Company

ISBN:	Hardcover	978-1-4828-3811-4
	Softcover	978-1-4828-3810-7
	eBook	978-1-4828-3809-1

To order additional copies of this book, contact
Partridge India
000 800 10062 62
orders.india@partridgepublishing.com

www.partridgepublishing.com/india

PREFACE

This novel is dedicated to my Best Friend Ajinkya. I always feel inspired when I see him.

I have used his name for the lead character of this novel as they both share some similar good qualities, which imprints a strong impact on the novel.

This story is inspired from the real world. If and when the characters and situations shown in the story seem real or familiar, then it is just a co-incidence.

Child Labour, Child sex abuse, and domestic violence is a curse to Humanity. So please don't encourage such crimes & don't let anyone do!

Smoking is injurious to health, and causes cancer.

Gourab Mitra

"Sometimes,
Even A Kid can Become your Teacher!"
- Gourab Mitra.

"You are essentially who you create yourself
to be and all that occurs in your life is
the result of your own making."
Stephen Richards

SINCERE THANKS

To

MEERA,

VISHAL GORDE, JAYANT ACHARYA.

&

My Mentors

MRS. KUMKUM MITRA (MA)

&

LATE MRS. NILIMA SINHA (DIDA)

Front Cover Illustration by

OM PRAKASH KHIRODKAR

A story inspired
by
real incidences

2015

One

Flat No 12, Nilima Housing Society,
Natubaug, Near Swargate,
Pune.

Kiran stepped out of the washroom. As she stood before the dressing table, she viewed herself anew. She gazed at the water droplets on her fair skin. They reminded her of the early morning dew on a freshly opened flower.

She dropped the towel down from her breasts and wiped the streamline of water running down her neck. "Beautiful! I have maintained an hourglass figure; slim and trim. My skin has the glow of a snake's skin! I have a healthy, soft body, with a round face, a flat stomach and full breasts."

As Kiran unwrapped the towel around her head and let her hair run down to touch her waist-line, she said, "Prefect! Ready for the first day of RJ! Welcome to Radio Rocks, RJ Kiran Kulkarni!"

She rubbed her straight long hair with the towel and then brushed it softly.

She suddenly looked at the wall-clock in the mirror and exclaimed, "It's 9 AM!"

She put down the brush and picked the dress kept on the bed. The bed was aligned in front of the dressing table.

Ten minutes later, dressed smartly, she went to the kitchen and prepared a cup of lemon grass tea. She poured the tea from the teapot into the cup and carried the cup of tea back to the hall.

She then removed her laptop from the bag and kept it on the bed and logged on to Facebook.

She could see updates of her friends and glanced at them. Suddenly the chatting window popped up. Prashant Bhurewar said, 'Hi ☺'

Kiran replied 'Hi ☺'

Prashant replied 'So 1st day of ur dream job How r u feeling?'

'I m hyper excited!!!!!' She replied.

'Dnt wrry i ll drop u ☺'

'no thanx...dnt wrry i ll manage'

He replied 'f9 ☺'

He then inquired, 'Well u did not answer my question yesterday'

She inquired, 'Which 1???'

He replied 'Will u marry me?'

She went blank and couldn't reply him. He again inquired, 'do u luv me?'

She replied, 'yes i do...but i need some tym ☺'

He immediately went offline. She then went into Omkar Kale's account.

His status was updated as: 'Pune i m cuming bak 2day!!!'

She mumured "He is my love, but past seven years we never had a word with each other. God knows where we will land up!"

And then she logged off.

Her breasts swelled with pride. By now, the tea had turned into cold sugar syrup. She left it at its place

"I am feeling like a new born baby today; the whole world seems new for me! I am unable to recognize anyone here! It's not the first time that I am in this city, or in this flat!"

"My mum had thought me, when I was a kid that –

Two personas live within us. One the Gigantic Good, and the other being The Devil. It's we who render the power to one, to overshadow the other; And that's what we become! AJ represents the first; and Javed represented the other!"

"This is the same flat where AJ and I lived years before. AJ!" she recalled.

She smiled and flagged him as her first love in her dark black eyes. My first love!" she said in a soft romantic voice.

In past ten to fifteen years, I never bothered to give so much time to myself. But, today it's my day! This day has come after a long wait. I have to look special and admirable," she murmured.

She sat in front of the mirror admired her own self. She took care of each and everything; right from her hair till her toes. She had arranged everything last night itself.

Her red and white churidar with beautiful hand work done on the whole set looked stunning on her. She draped the white dupatta on it.

Cosmetics added a touch of glamour to her beauty. She left her long, lustrous black hair open and kept the hair clip in her purse.

She looked at her appointment letter kept on the dressing table. It had a watermark of Radio Rocks on the bottom left hand corner. She had to reach office by 11 AM.

"I need to hurry up!"

She got up and went into her room, took her purse and the folder. She kept the letter in the folder. She kept a white handkerchief and some makeup stuff in her purse. She zipped up the purse and slung the bag around her right shoulder.

She then went into the hall, kept her purse on the table; she sat on the chair and wore her new, black sandals with pencil heels. She picked up her purse and moved out, taking care to lock the house properly.

Her beautiful designer wrist watch showed 10 am.

She walked to the main road. From here her office was at a distance of forty minutes.

She went to the other side of the road. She saw the bus stop nearby and walked towards it. A huge crowd of children, youth and senior people were standing at the bus stop, anxiously awaiting for their respective buses. When it did come, the crowd surged forward, pushing and rushing and Kiran was left out.

She asked an aged person, "When is the next bus for Swargate?" He stared at her from top to bottom, gave her a weird look and then replied, "Do I look like government employee who works for PMPML! Check the board!" He pointed to the LED board. The board displayed the time-table. Kiran blushed with embarrassment and muttered to herself, "Attitude ah! Shh!"

She looked around. A couple of young guys were staring at her. She now started feeling uncomfortable and pulled her dress down as if to cover her exposed body. She shifted her handbag from the right shoulder to the left. But they were still staring at her!

She murmured, "Enough! Let me move!"

She walked ahead hoping to catch an auto-rickshaw. She looked around for one when a rickshaw came her way. She waved for it to stop. She looked inside the rickshaw; there was no one on the back seat. She inquired, "Bhaiya! Swargate?"

"Yes, but will go by meter!"

"Take some more passengers?" she suggested.

"No! Rules are rules!" he replied.

In the absence of any other vehicle and with precious minutes ticking away, she had no other choice but to take this rickshaw. The driver shifted the meter down and they moved ahead.

Kiran suddenly felt cold. She looked around and murmured again "But it's a sunny day today. So weird?"

Was it a little nervousness before her dream job took off?

She gently rubbed her palms.

TWO

The auto-rickshaw crawled ahead in the peak hour traffic. Kiran's thoughts raced too. Sometimes excited, sometimes nervous, sometimes confident, and sometimes full of doubts. Her hair flew over her eyes, momentarily blinding her. She hastened to move it behind her ears.

And then they were there. She looked at her wrist watch. 10:18!

She got down, looked at driver. He said, "Twenty Rupees!"

She opened her purse, paid the fare demanded by the rickshaw-driver and didn't even look at the meter, much to the driver's delight.

Kiran looked around for a sweet-mart. She saw one located in a small building on the ground floor. She walked in and looked at the sweets displayed in the showcase; Maharashtrian sweets, Bengali sweets, Gujrati sweets. The sweet-mart was vast. There were only about a dozen customers in the shop but there was no space to walk!

She said, "Oh bhaiya, come here!"

A guy came to her. She pointed towards the showcase and asked, 'Oh bhaiya, which sweet is the best one here?'

He answered, 'madam, this is a reputed sweet-mart and all sweets are excellent!'

She glanced at him. He was wearing a maroon sleeveless vest and blue coloured pants. He had a dirty white napkin on his shoulder. His hair was wet with sweat.

He inquired, Which one do you want?'

'Oh God! Help me! There are so many sweets around me. If you ask my wish, I would buy all of them!' She was confused about what to buy and what not. She looked at her watch. She pointed to the tray of white peda.

He asked, 'one kilo?'

She scratched her head for a while and then said, 'fine!'

He went in. He picked up an empty box from a shelf and then took the tray out. He started picking up the pedas, weighed them. When the weight machine showed, '997 grams', he stopped dropping pedas into the box.

Kiran murmured, 'kanjus!'

"Bhaiya put some more!"

He looked at her with protest and dropped one peda and closed the box. He pointed towards the counter and said and said "Pay there!"

After what seemed like an eternity, Kiran walked out of shop. A few yards away was the office building where she had to report! It looked so old and ordinary; she wondered whether it was really where she had to go. She looked into the letter again to confirm the address mentioned, it had the name of this building. She climbed the stairs and walked to the lift. There were three people before her in the queue. They went into the lift and Kiran followed them.

There was a lift-operator in a blue uniform.

Kiran was overcome with doubts.

"How will be nature of my colleagues? What if someone doesn't like this sweet?"

Her heart impatiently popped up. It said, "Relax! Don't be hyper!"

She closed her eyes. She started reciting the Gayatri Mantra.

She chanted, "Om bhur bhuvasavah tatsavitur avrenya bharogh devasya dhimahi dhiyo yonah prachodayat!"

Suddenly, the lift stopped. The crowd moved out from that congested box. She followed the crowd in the way to go out of the lift. The liftman looked at her. He inquired, "Where are you going?"

She stopped at the edge of the lift. She replied him in an excited voice, "Radio Rocks!"

He quickly replied back, "Two floors up!"

She moved back into the lift. He looked at her from top to bottom. He saw the box of sweets. A question-mark flashed on his old skinny face.

He inquired, "New RJ?"

She was taken back and replied with a happy voice, "Yes!"

"I didn't expect that from a lift-man!" Then an idea clicked in her mind. 'Let's offer him a sweet!"

Suddenly a message popped up in her brain.

'What will the office people think? Is someone in this lift from your office? He is a lift-man!' her brain countered

She raised her hand to open the box and then she moved her hand back!

He saw her playing with the sweet box. His face showed disappointment.

The lift reached Third floor - Radio Rocks floor.

She looked at him. He looked at her with an attitude. He said, “Move! That’s your office.” He pointed and protested, “I am on duty! And I am busy!”

She moved out of the lift. She didn’t like the way he spoke to her. But she knew the reason behind it!

She approached the reception. A thin young woman with lots of make-up on her face was sitting on the chair of receptionist.

“She looks disgusting!” Kiran said to herself.

Kiran walked to her desk, and gave her the appointment letter from her folder. She read it and returned it to Kiran.

The receptionist forwarded a register to her. She requested “Make an entry in this register!”

She filled in the info required in the register- her name, contact number, etc. She signed in the last column and returned the register. The receptionist said, “Please deposit the cell-phone there!”

She pointed to the mobile counter. Kiran was asked to fill details there as well in the register. She was then given a Temporary I-card.

"Uff! There are too many formalities!"

She was asked to take a seat, she sat on the couch. The receptionist picked the receiver. She dialed a number on the keypad.

Sometime later, a thin office boy came out. He called, "Kiran Kulkarni!" He looked around. She got up. He said, "You have come as RJ?"

"Yes!"

"Our manager has called you! Follow me!"

Kiran said, "Yes!" She looked at the receptionist who was busy answering a phone call and went in.

Ah! Fully centralized air-conditioning office! People were busy working on computers. Some of them glanced at her. "I am not an alien! Why are they staring at me?"

She started feeling awkward. She tried to ignore her nervousness.

A second later, "It means I am looking beautiful!"

They walked to the Manager's cabin. He knocked on the door and went in. A minute later he came out.

He said, "The Manager has called you in. Go!" he said and he left. Kiran went in.

The Manager was sitting on his chair. He was fat and bald headed and around 38 to 40 years old. The Manager got up and congratulated her. He said, "Have a seat!"

He offered her a glass of water and she felt better. Sometime later, he asked, "Would you like to have tea or coffee?"

Kiran looked confused "What should I say? Yes, or should I say no? How will he feel?"

After thinking for a while, she declined. And at the same time she opened the box and offered him sweets.

"Follow me! I will show you the office!"

Kiran closed the box and got up and followed him. He took her around the office. He said, "There are numerous departments in the office. Let's go to all the sections of the office!"

The manager was very friendly and charming! They spoke like friends and that's when she came out of her comfort zone! She got to see each and every department. They later went into the conference room. They sat. He said "Be seated here! Soon RJ Sameer will come here! You have to assist him!"

He got up and walked to the door. He left; and now Kiran was all alone in the conference room. She shrieked in the soft cushion chair. She looked out of the window to her left.

The light blue clouds were dancing with the wind under the bright sky. The bright yellow sun was smiling at her. She could see the road and the crowd. At the corner of the road, there was a small tea stall.

She sat back on the chair. Slowly, she started recollecting a past story. And a cloud covered the bright sun.

JANUARY 2004

THREE

It was a cold night waiting to turn into dawn. Tongue-biting cold in fact! There was darkness everywhere, the moon and the sun were busy playing hide and seek!

A short-haired, pale skinned child was sleeping exposed to the universe. He seemed to be enjoying his sleep on his bed, which was the hard tar of the road with pebbles and his bed sheet was the dust over it. He was dressed in black shorts and a blue half- shirt, torn in some places.

Surprisingly, the child's face seemed peaceful, like that of a yogi lying on a bed of nails.

Salim came out of the tent. He saw Kiran sleeping happily. He looked around. He shouted "Javed? Javed?"

But no reply came back his way. Javed was coming slowly. He was visible at a distance.

He said "Bhenchod! Get up!" and he kicked vessels around. The loud noise travelled into Kiran's creative dream world. And his world crashed down in seconds.

Kiran started crying with pain. Javed heard his loud noise and he rushed to the spot. He saw Kiran crying. He rolled on his bed. Javed halted a few meters away.

Javed had gone to collect Fresh Cream Rolls from the nearby Bakery.

Salim left. Javed looked at him with anger. He went back to the stall and kept the packet of cream roll.

Javed went to Kiran. He lifted him by holding up his shoulders. He wiped his eyes with his palms. Kiran wailed loudly. Javed held him in his arms. He interwened lips with Kiran's.

Javed pulled Kiran's lips in and a sour juice flew in Javed's mouth. And Javed transferred a sweet juice of Hope into his mouth. Seeing this whole drama, the moon vanished.

FOUR

On the other side of the road, stood a five - storey tall Business Complex made of Glass.

On the 3rd Floor of the building was located Hands on Venture. It was an International Outbound Business Process Outsourced. In short a BPO.

There were two night shifts which the company ran. Shift One - 5:30 PM to 1:30 AM and Shift two - 1:30 AM to 9:30 AM; there was another shift which was a mid-shift.

Mid-shift ended around 6:00 AM.

The people living far away were provided with transport facility. There are almost 15 people working in mid-shift.

It was 6:25 AM, the mid-shift has finished. The mid-shift people started moving out from the building. Among them were, Ajinkya Jadhav, Rahul Kale and Krishna Patel.

They lived nearby. The group of three friends was part of same Portfolio and they worked mid-shift.

Today, they decided to have a sip of tea at the tea stall opposite the road. They crossed the road and went to the tea stall.

But there was no one there. They looked around, but didn't find anyone.

Rahul said, "Guys let's be seated. The chaiwala will be somewhere around! Let's relax, he will be back!"

Krishna giggled and said, "Nice place for time-pass!"

There was a plastic table and a wooden bench placed in front of the stall. Rahul and Krishna sat on the wooden bench. Ajinkya went to the stall and searched for a cigarette. He found one kept in a carton.

Rahul shouted, "Get one for me as well!"

Ajinkya, the quietest guy didn't say anything. He lit the cigarette and sat on the bench. Ajinkya gave Rahul the cigarette.

When, after a cigarette butted, they were planning to light another, Kiran came out of the tent and a moment later Javed followed.

Their lips were red and moist.

They rubbed their faces on their arms. Kiran looked down. Javed ran to the stove.

Krishna said, "Hey this stall is run by kids! Amazing yaar, self-dependant kids ah!"

Kiran raised his eyes up with protest.

Rahul interrupted Krishna, said to the kids, "Fast man. Three cutting chai and six cream rolls!"

Krishna said, "Let's have one, if it's good we will take one more." Rahul agreed.

Krishna replied, "God knows how many days old it is!"

Javed said with attitude, "Pay first and then we will serve you!" and he pumped the stove.

Krishna looked at him, got up and went near him. He looked at him again. Javed gave him attitude. Krishna pulled his wallet out of his pocket. He paid the money. Kiran took it. Krishna inquired, "But can you really prepare tea? You will not burn yourself? Are you sure?"

Kiran looked at Krishna with anger. Krishna commented on his look, "Checkout his looks! 3 foot spike kid and see his six foot attitude. Ha! Ha!"

Rahul commented, "They are running this stall, so they might be aware about it! It's his job!"

Rahul got up. He took three cream rolls. He gave one to Ajinkya and one to Krishna.

Javed poured the tea in small glass cups. Kiran served the tea to them. Kiran went to Ajinkya.

He took the cup from Kiran's small hands.

He asked Kiran, "What's your name?"

Kiran answered "Kiran."

Krishna busted with laughter. Ajinkya stared at Krishna.

"What happened?" enquired Rahul in a sleepy tone.

"K...K...Kiran. Do you remember Shah Rukh Khan in Darr! Oh my God, my stomach is paining now. I can't help it!"

Ajinkya smiled. Rahul kept his cup down and laughed. Kiran dropped his head down. The fire of anger flashed in his eyes.

Ajinkya looked at him. He commanded Krishna, "Shh!"

Everyone was numb. Ajinkya said to Kiran, "Don't mind! He is mad!"

Kiran didn't reply. Ajinkya said, "It is better to leave! Let's move!"

Rahul picked another three cream rolls and half a packet of cigarettes. He paid Javed. And they left.

They walked down the street. Rahul and Ajinkya left Krishna at his place. And then they walked for a few minutes. They reached a circle. They took the road to their left. About a five minute walk, they reached the end of the road. There were two apartments facing each other where the road ended.

Ajinkya lived in Nilima Housing Society and Rahul in Vandhan Housing Society. A metal bench was placed next to the gate of Ajinkya's apartment building.

Rahul and Ajinkya sat on the bench. They started chatting. Ajinkya lit a cigarette. He took a puff and he passed it to Rahul.

About 7 minute later, the cigarette butted. Rahul offered a toffee to Ajinkya. Rahul had one too.

A minute later, Rahul's mother came to the window. Rahul looked at her.

Rahul said, "Now Omkar will leave for the school. My mom has come to the window." He looked at his wrist watch, and he said, "7 in the morning! One more day is over!"

Omkar walked down the stairs of his apartment building. He has dressed in a sky blue half- shirt and Prussian blue shorts, which was his school uniform; a white colour tie, was also part of his uniform and black socks with black shoes.

A heavily loaded school bag was slung on his small shoulders. He was carrying a Tiffin bag in his right hand and a big Milton water bottle in his left hand.

He looked back towards the window. His mother was eagerly standing to see him board the bus safely. She gave him a flying kiss. He took it and returned it with two. He looked ahead and started walking.

When he had walked a small distance, he found an empty plastic bottle. He started playing football with it. He then realized that someone was sitting on the brown bench. He looked up. He saw Ajinkya and Rahul sitting on the bench. He smiled and walked to them.

Ajinkya smiled at him. He inquired, “In which standard are you Omkar?”

He thought for a while and then counted something on his fingers. Ajinkya looked at his tie, which had the initials of the school imprinted on it.

And he answered, “This is the fifth time, you’re asking this same question this month!” He took a deep breath. “Ok Fine! This is the last time I’m telling you this! I’m in 5th

Standard. Next time, you ask me this same question, you will have to give me a Cadbury. Remember!"

Ajinkya replied, "I am sorry. I forgot!"

He took out his right hand from the pocket. His palm was closed.

"But here is your Cadbury!"

He opened his palm and offered a Cadbury. Omkar quickly picked it up and shouted with joy, "Thanks bhaiya!"

He tore the chocolate wrapper from one end. A spark flashed in his eyes. He took a bite and he felt happy.

He enjoyed the chocolate. He was lost in the chocolate. Rahul took advantage of this. Slowly he took his hand close to him. He pulled his pant down. He screamed on top of his voice. Ajinkya smiled watching their Tom and Jerry fight. His mom shouted, "Rahul!"

Rahul bit his tongue and Omkar pulled his pant up. The school-bus arrived at the corner. He walked to the bus quietly. He looked at his mom and climbed the steps. The helper closed the door and the bus left. Mom went in.

Rahul said, "Chalo, I will take your leave now! Need to attend Mom's lecture."

He shook hand with Ajinkya. Ajinkya smiled.

Rahul said, "I have seen you smile after a week. I was waiting for this!"

The smile disappeared from Ajinkya's face.

Rahul said, "Keep smiling. You inspire many!"

Rahul left. He walked towards his apartment. Suddenly he stopped.

He came back. He inquired, "You had gone to the hospital? How is she?"

"Yes." He replied with sadness in his voice. "But there is no improvement!"

Rahul tapped his shoulder. He smiled. He consoled Ajinkya, "Don't worry everything will be fine! Don't loose hope! This world exists on hope!"

Rahul walked towards his apartment.

Rahul lived with his parents and his younger brother Omkar. But Ajinkya Jadhav lived alone in a 1BHK flat.

Ajinkya was left alone on the metal bench. He kept quiet.

It's said that whenever you're alone, you either travel back into your Past, or else you live in the Future! You cannot live in Present!

He too travelled to his past by the time machine! The sun slowly moved up.

The Sun slowly started moving higher and higher in the sky.

Kiran and Javed went back to their routine. Many people came and went. Their day started on a bad note, but it ended well.

The sun was slowly setting in the west. The city-hall clock struck 4'o clock!

A school bus stood at the corner of the road. The door opened. Omkar had come back from the school. The time today was good for him, he enjoyed his day! Oh, it had to be good because it had begun with the bite of chocolate! He had a smile on his face. He waved his hand to say goodbye to all his friends!

He was tired. Sweat running down on his red cheeks. He was carrying the school bag on his shoulder and Tiffin bag in his hand. He found an empty bottle fallen at the corner of the road. He kicked it. He started playing football with that bottle. He came near the apartment gate. He realized that someone was there on the bench. He turned back and he saw Ajinkya sleeping on the bench. He walked to the bench and he looked at him. He kept his Tiffin bag down on the ground. He kept his bag on the corner of the bench. He sat on the bench near his head.

Ajinkya was wearing the same shirt and jeans pant which he had worn early morning today. The Dirt formed an outline of his clothes! After long months today he was saw Ajinkya sleeping in peace! Otherwise he was always tense and had a run around act!. Omkar didn't knew the reason for that but he was always concerned about Ajinkya!

Omkar shared all his problems with him. But he never inquired about it! Rather he never liked to hurt him by refreshing his pain!

Omkar always was busy. They only met in the morning. Ajinkya helped him in his studies during the weekends.

Omkar moved his hand over Ajinkya's dusty hair. A cool breeze ran in his brain. Ajinkya opened his eyes.

Ajinkya looked at his black square-shaped wrist watch. He smiled and said, Hey you're back?"

Omkar remained quiet. Omkar removed his handkerchief from his pocket and wiped his face. Ajinkya had become black like a burnt chocolate cake!

Omkar said, "Bhaiya you didn't go home? You're still here!"

Ajinkya got up. Omkar picked up his school bag and Tiffin bag.

Omkar said, "Let's go home!"

He followed Ajinkya. Ajinkya moved towards his apartment. Omkar caught his wrist. He said, "Let's have a cup of tea!"

Ajinkya looked back. Omkar pointed towards his house. He took him to his house. Omkar's mother was happy seeing him here.

She greeted him. She said, "You have come home after many months!"

Omkar said, "He did not come! I brought him here!"

He sat his tired body on the wooden chair. She went in the kitchen. She was busy cooking dinner.

Omkar went into his room, kept his bag on the table. He then kept the Tiffin bag in kitchen. He said, "He was sleeping on the bench!"

And then, he went back to his room to change. Mother came to the hall. She gave Ajinkya a glass of water. She said, "Go and wash your face! You will feel better!"

He stretched his face to give her a smile. But he failed. He went to the basin. He washed his face and wiped it with the small towel hanging on the rod, below the basin.

Omkar threw his shirt on the bed. He went in the washroom. Ajinkya went in the bedroom. He saw Rahul sleeping in peace. He has wrapped the blanket around him like a silk-worm packed in the cocoon. He went into Omkar's room.

He saw his school shirt lying on the bed. He picked it up and folded it. He opened the cupboard. He kept it with the other shirts.

Suddenly, mother shouted, "Omkar why didn't you eat the vegetable?"

Omkar replied from the washroom, "Mom I hate carrot. You know!"

His voice echoed. The running tap added the background music to this healthy conversation.

She replied with a rise in her voice, "But that's good for eyes!"

Omkar opened the door and came out. Omkar, "Mom please!"

He went to his room. She turned back. Ajinkya was standing at the entrance of the kitchen. She kept quiet.

The tea pot kept on the gas had water boiling in it. It was shouting, "Hey prepare the tea or else I will evaporate!"

She had the Tiffin in her hand. One was empty and the other had the vegetables left untouched by Omkar.

Mother smiled looking at Ajinkya. She said calmly, "Child, have a seat!"

"No aunty that's fine!" he replied.

Omkar wore a blue coloured checked half-shirt and a maroon half- pant. He combed his hair and applied some powder on the face. He went in the hall and sat on the couch. He placed his legs over couch.

He switched on the T.V. Ajinkya came in the hall. Omkar dragged his feet down from the couch. Ajinkya sat next to him. He switched to Cartoon Network. Mother came in the hall carrying a tray and a cup of tea and a supandi mug. She said 'have a cup of tea!"

He picked the small cup. She went to Omkar. She offered him the chocolate flavoured milk in his favourite Supandi mug.

Ajinkya inquired, "Aunty your cup?"

She replied with a smile, "I will have it sometime later!"

She whispered, "After you're finished take him with you, or else he and Rahul will start fighting."

Ajinkya replied, "Fine!" And he took a sip.

"Omkar is too naughty! Now see he will slowly increase the volume! Rahul is tired and is sill sleeping. Omkar will break his sleep!"

Ajinkya smiled and took a sip. She went in and she got back to her work.

Ajinkya said, “Omkar, let’s go home!”

“Ya you go home!”

“You have to come with me!” Ajinkya said. He kept the glass on the dining table.

“Ajinkya commanded,“Carry your books as well!”

“Hmm!”

Omkar went in the bed room. He opened was school bag. He checked his calendar. He took the books he required and the compass box. He came in the hall.

“Let’s move!” he said.

They walked down the stairs. They reached the parking.

“So Bhaiya! How was your collection?”

Ajinkya looked at him and reacted, “Can you change the topic?”

They reached their destination. He unlocked his house. They went in. Omkar switched on the T.V. set. Ajinkya looked at him. He said, “Switch off the T.V.!”

“Bhaiya! Tired of studies! Please!”

Ajinkya kept quiet. He shrieked in the couch.

FIVE

The sun was again lazy today. His light was not carrying heat with it. A cold air was flowing with the wind. Many trees have shed their leaves and have decorated the surrounding. The flowers have bloomed. The smell of different flowers amused everyone around. This was the signal that, the winter has arrived.

Rahul and Krishna came late at the tea stall around 7am. Usually they arrived at 6:30 am. Both of them looked tired and stressed. They were very quiet, as if they had smelt a snake, or as if they had arrived from a funeral. And today Ajinkya was missing. They ordered, "2 teas and 2 cream rolls!"

Kiran inquired, "No cigarette today?"

Krishna said, "We have it with us!"

Kiran looked around. He thought maybe Ajinkya was late.

Rahul said, "Today's day was very bad!" Rahul removed the cigarette from the case. Krishna lit the cigarette with his lighter. He took a puff and he gave it to him. They sat down.

Kiran served them tea and cream rolls.

Rahul replied, "Thanks! I really required this!"

Krishna looked at him. He inquired, "What happened?"

Rahul drove the smoke out. He said, "I firstly did not give a cent collection. And then I had a quarrel with one of the neighbours in my society before my shift. It spoiled my mood completely!"

He took a puff. He continued, "Today's day was bad. Rather it was the worst day!"

Javed was removing the dirt collected around the stove; Kiran was pretending of doing some work, but he was eagerly listening to their conversation. Kiran waited for a while but he couldn't see Ajinkya coming.

Kiran murmured, "Why am I feeling the absence of Ajinkya? Why?"

He travelled in the past. He recollected, "Yes! He was the only who has never made fun of me! He is the only one who understands me! Meeting him is now a part of my daily routine! And I know him since three weeks!"

Kiran gazed around. He then looked at them. He later murmured again, "Where is he? He has still not come!"

Kiran slowly became impatient. He broke his silence. He inquired, "Where is Ajinkya Bhaiya today?"

Rahul replied, "He has gone to the hospital!"

Kiran questioned him back "Why? Is he fine?"

Krishna looked at him with surprise.

Rahul looked at Krishna. He took a puff and then answered, "Well, yes! He is fine!"

Kiran doubted, "Something is wrong! He is hiding something from me!"

Kiran kept quiet. They finished their tea and cream rolls and then they left. And Javed and Kiran got back to their daily routine.

It was nine according to the city clock tower. The darkness of the night had spread all over. There was no rush at the tea stall today. Kiran was sitting down on his knees and busy washing the chores. He saw a known person coming towards his tea stall.

Who is he? I feel like I know him!"

Soon, he recognized him.

"Hey! That's Ajinkya!" Kiran said in an excited voice.

He was dressed in a black leather coat. He came to the tea stall. He sat on the big rock. Javed went in to see whether the rice was cooked! Kiran got up. He smiled.

Kiran inquired, "Hey bhaiya how are you?"

Ajinkya replied, "I'm fine! What about you?"

Kiran replied, "Fine!"

Kiran continued, "I heard you went to hospital, but you look fine?"

Ajinkya replied, "No I am fine."

He kept quiet for a moment, and then said "I had work in the hospital. So I went there directly from work!"

But his face revealed his tiredness; still he has put on the mask of a smiling face. He opened the cigarette case from his pocket. He looked at Kiran.

Kiran's shirt was wet with sweat. Ajinkya could smell his sweat. His face had turned red like a piece of roasted chicken. His face expressed various emotions. One of them was stress and the other was of happiness. His hand has become hard like the buffalo's skin.

Ajinkya picked a cigarette from the case. He rushed his hand into his pocket. He removed the lighter and lit it.

Ajinkya ordered for cream roll! Kiran served him a cup of tea. Ajinkya took the glass from him. He took a sip of the hot tea. He closed his eyes. He comprehended, "Ah! Good tea!"

The lines of stress reduced from his forehead. Kiran resumed his work. Ajinkya looked at him. He saw him washing utensils.

Ajinkya asked, "Kiran you're washing utensils?"

Kiran looked at him. He continued, "When will you study?"

Kiran answered with a sad voice, "Bhaiya, I am not so lucky, to go to school!"

Ajinkya thought for a moment. He then questioned, "So where is your family?"

Kiran replied, "I have no one! That's the reason I am working for bread and butter!"

Ajinkya kept quiet for a moment. He thought for a moment and inquired, "So where do you live?"

Kiran pointed to the tent. Ajinkya got a shock.

Ajinkya asked agitatedly, "Don't you feel cold? It's 6 degree!"

Kiran replied, "No option. I cannot do anything! I am all alone in this world!"

A message popped up in Ajinkya's mind, "Hey I too!"

Something stuck in his throat. He wanted to speak something, but he struggled to speak as if he was dumb. Ajinkya looked at him.

Ajinkya took a sip of the hot tea. His heart said, "Hey Ajinkya! You need to help him!"

He countered, "Forget it! Why do I have to do? I have lots of problems in my life already!"

Kiran looked at the tense face Ajinkya and Kiran quickly changed the topic.

Kiran said, "Why are you tense?"

Ajinkya kept quiet. Kiran said, "Tension will not solve your problems! It will only block your thinking!"

Ajinkya kept quiet. Kiran said, "I want to go to the school. I studied till fourth. But for bread and butter I am working. No one is ready to give me admission."

"Why?"

"No guardian!"

Kiran kept quiet. Ajinkya took another sip. Kiran continued, "You're listening this is RJ. He is my favourite! I wanna be like him!"

RJ Subodh announced, "This is my favourite track from the movie, Kal Ho Na Ho! Friends feel it! Today's end mantra 'World begins with you and ends with you; so things happen with your will and desire!' On this beautiful note I am leaving you tonight! Shabakher!"

Ajinkya looked at Kiran. He saw a spark in Kiran's eyes. He had the frustration in his eyes. He sounded like he was begging to Ajinkya, 'Help me!'

Ajinkya could feel it. But he was confused how to help Kiran? He looked at the brown cold sugar syrup. He took a sip. Kiran read his face.

Kiran said, "Don't worry! My good days will also come. Like ways, your good days will be back. Where there is a will, there is a way!"

Ajinkya looked at him. Kiran smiled. Ajinkya took a last sip. He got up charged. He kept the cup on the glass board cupboard. He paid him the charges. He left to go to the office.

He hummed, "Har pal yahan jeebhar jeeo jo hai sama kal ho na ho!"

SIX

Experimental Tea

It's a Sunday today. It's a day of enjoyment for everyone!

It's just 6 in the morning. The kids were playing cricket on the ground. And Kiran was watching them from the tea stall. They were barely visible. The ground was far from the tea stall. And there was no Sunday for Kiran and Javed.

In fact, that's the most important day of business. Even without the call centre crowd they still managed to do a good business every Sunday!

Many office-going people go for a walk early morning. Some people were doing their routine exercise. Some were running from one end to another of the ground. After they finished their exercise, they like to have a cup of tea.

Kiran murmured, "Playing on the ground is a nightmare for me!"

He dropped his face down. Today he was busy in work. He had to service his customers. And today's main news was Kiran had to prepare the tea on his own today!

He murmured. "Have I prepared it well? Will the customers like it? If not, Salim will beat me again with the brown stick!"

He looked tense. He stirred the mixture with the tablespoon. The vessel containing the tea was warm.

The milky-brown colour is perfect, he said. He called, "Javed! Come fast!"

Javed says, "Yes?"

Kiran says, "Taste it!"

Kiran joined his palms and stretched them down to his navel. He closed his eyes. He prayed, "It should be good, or else this is a loss. And it will eat my today's wages and I will not be able to buy pastries! Please! Please God!!"

Javed taped his shoulder. He opened his eyes. Javed says, "Don't worry!"

Javed moved towards the stove. He stirred the mixture with the spoon first. He took a sip on his hand by a spoon. He tasted it.

He thought for a moment. Kiran looked at his emotionless face. Javed looked and said, "It is almost done!"

Kiran took a deep breath, "Ah!"

He continued, "Just need to boil for next two minutes! Get the glasses."

Kiran said "I am feeling better!"

Javed increased the flame. Kiran washed the glasses with soap water and later with normal water. He wiped the glasses with a piece of white cloth with red lines on it.

Javed reduced the flame He picked the vessel off the fire. Then he picked the vessel of coffee and kept it over. He served the tea to the customers.

One customer said, "Kiran, you prepared it well! You have magic in your hands!"

Kiran's work was appreciated by everyone. A smile popped up on Kiran's stressed face. The customers left.

Javed went in the tent. He called, "Kiran come in! I have some work with you!" Kiran went in. He caught Kiran's hand. He pulled him closer. Slowly the Desperate Devil became visible in his eyes. He slowly moved his hand on his shoulder; his warm hand reached the back. He locked Kiran in his firm arms. He looked in his eyes. Kiran looked down. Javed had always helped him so Kiran couldn't deny him his demand!

He caught Kiran's neck with his right hand; he pushed Kiran's face up. Javed's lips have turned red like a tomato; His eyes navigated top to bottom. He bent his neck to reach Kiran's lips and locked them.

Slowly Kiran started enjoying the moment. And suddenly there was a call for tea by a customer, like a commercial ad! It disturbed their memorable scene!

Kiran pulled himself out. He looked at Javed; Javed shook his head and said, "Don't leave me now!"

Kiran wanted to continue to live this moment, but a customer was on hold. The customer called, "Anyone there?"

Kiran's heart popped, "He is using you! Leave him!"

He debated, "No! He is not!"

The heart debated back, "Yes, he is! He is using you, because he knows your truth! Remember, the world knows Kiran is a boy; but the reality is something different!"

He was numb. He calmed himself. He moved back. He wiped his sweat. He took a deep breath. He looked at Javed and smiled. And he replied to the customer, "Yes coming!"

He wiped his face and said, "I enjoyed it!"" and ran out. Javed took time to calm down. He murmured "You are paying to me as I am hiding your secret!"

Seven

Ajinkya woke up. He looked at his big round wall-clock with his partially-opened eyes. "Its 10:40 am" he said. He got up. He went to the washroom. He washed his face. He came out. He sat in the hall. He got up and walked to the door. He opened the main door. He removed the newspaper stuck in the handle.

He walked back to the hall. He sat over the black old couch. He opened the newspaper and started reading it. He read couple of news from each page. After reading it, he folded and kept the newspaper on the centre-table.

He heard a knock at his door. Ajinkya looked towards the door. Omkar was standing at the entrance holding a tray in his hand. He was wearing a half pant and a blue checks half-shirt. He gave a smile to Ajinkya. Ajinkya replied with a smile.

He walked in. He kept the bowl on the centre-table and sat besides Ajinkya.

"So my best friend, how are you?"

"I am fine. What about you?"

"Boring life is going on."

"Why? What happened?"

"Nothing man. No girl-friend."

"Ok! That's the reason!"

"Well. I heard you had gone to the hospital, yesterday?"

"Yes. I did!"

"So how is she?"

"Yes!" with a numb voice.

"Oh! How romantic! God, when will I fall in love?"

Ajinkya's sad face displayed a smile. He nodded his head left and right.

"Mom has made chocolate cake with nuts and cashews. Let's have it! But first you have to prepare tea!"

"Ok!" said Ajinkya.

Ajinkya went in the kitchen. Omkar sat on the platform.

Ajinkya inquired, "Help me!"

He replied, "I will do supervision!"

Ajinkya nodded his head. He said "So how are your studies going?"

Omkar replied, "Doing well. Soon my studies will bring exams. Don't ask boring questions!"

Ajinkya started laughing.

Omkar said, "Waiter add ginger to it and make it a bit strong."

Ajinkya turned towards him. He smashed a fight on his right arm.

"So how was your football match?" Ajinkya inquired, "And how many goals did you score?"

"I was the main person of the team!"

"Ok! What were you playing as? Forward or Goal-keeper?"

"No. I was playing as an extra player. I was their trump card!"

"Oh I see!" Ajinkya commented.

"If everyone plays, who will cheer the team!" he replied.

"Hmm!"

"It was boring! Bodily F...!" replied Omkar with aggression.

"Ok!" Ajinkya giggled, "You mean to say you didn't get a chance to play!"

"Ah! Laugh man. I saw your friendship. Ah! Focus on the tea. It's almost done. I am waiting in the balcony. Get the tea as well as the chocolate cake!"

He went in the balcony. He sat over the wooden jute chair. Ajinkya brought the tea in balcony. A plastic white table was kept in the corner. He pulled it in front and kept the tea over it. He went in the hall and picked the tray. He brought it in the balcony.

Omkar was busy playing video game. Ajinkya commented instantly, "You're so mean! Couldn't even get the cake here while coming?"

Omkar replied him, "That's how I reacted on my captain. If I would have got a chance to play, I would have impressed at least one girl!"

Ajinkya was tired of his constant cry for a girl-friend. He said, "Cut the crap!"

Omkar noticed the stress lines on Ajinkya's face. Omkar picked his mug that had Supandi printed on it. It's his favourite mug. He would never even drink water in a normal glass. He requires Supandi mug. Ajinkya picked his mug.

Omkar took a sip. He picked up a piece of cake. He took a bit of it. He looked at Ajinkya. Ajinkya was tense and very serious. Behind his head, there was something which was eating him up. Earlier Omkar felt it was the normal stress which he always has! Ajinkya took a sip. The stress lines fainted, but did not disappear. He was lost in his own thoughts. Then, Omkar realized, this is something different!

Omkar asked, "What's wrong my friend? I suppose something is going in your mind!"

Ajinkya kept quiet. He took a deep breath. He then took a sip. And he started, "You're very lucky!"

Omkar inquired, "What? How can you say that?" Omkar looked at him with an emotionless face.

Ajinkya continued, "I saw a kid at a tea-stall. It is opposite my office. He is of your age. You're enjoying your life, your childhood! The reason is, your parents are working and earning. They are fulfilling your desires! But I see him working for his bread and butter! That's why; he has compromised with his childhood! The reason is he has no one in this big world! But still he has hopes that one day everything will change! Something good will happen for him! He lives on the road! He gets beatings as his breakfast! He wants to study, but to survive he has to work! So, he has compromised with his education. He wants to become a RJ! He is small, but still has big dreams! I can see a power in his eyes. He hates his life; still he wants to change it! I wanna to help him! But I am confused how to help him?"

Ajinkya took another sip. He stretched his hand to grab a piece of cake. But he found the bowl empty. He looked at Omkar. Omkar is busy having the last piece of cake.

He looked at Ajinkya. He offered him a bite. Ajinkya ate the cake by Omkar's hand. Omkar's fingers are coated with a layer of cake. Omkar licked his fingers one by one.

Omkar took a sip of tea. He went to the wash-basin. He came back. He took a sip of tea again. He started, "Good! Appreciated!"

Ajinkya smiled.

Omkar continued, "Good cake!" Ajinkya kept quiet. He looked at Ajinkya. He changed the topic. He replied like Grandfather, "Well, you have a good desire! We should do something!"

Omkar started thinking. He sat down. He tapped his head with his fingers. He got up. He walked from one corner to another.

Almost after five minutes he snapped his fingers with joy. Ajinkya wondered what this little boy could do in this?

Omkar said, "This is a big house. Why don't you bring him here! Take his responsibility!"

Ajinkya reacted with shock, "What? How?"

Such numerous questions popped into his mind instantly.

Omkar looked at Ajinkya. He showed a Red Signal and indicated to hold on. Omkar explained, "Well you live alone Right?"

"Right!" Ajinkya replied.

"He has no one in his family! Correct?" he inquired.

"Right! So?"

"You can take his responsibility!" he said.

"Ya! But how can I bring him here?" Ajinkya inquired.

"You should bring him here. Let me explain something to you! If you take care of his education, he will have to give less time to his job. This will be disliked by the stall owner. You said he beats him; He will get another reason for that. By this, he might quit his studies!"

"That's true!" Ajinkya agreed.

He continued,

"If you bring him here, you can take up his studies and I can help him! Your loneliness will vanish! Taking care of children doesn't mean only paying fees or giving clothes! It means you need to live with them as children! Teach him good things. Reduce his bad habits and slowly they will disappear from him. Encourage him and motivate him to live his life in a better way!"

Ajinkya admired him by rolling his black eyeballs.

He continued,

"You will discover his good and bad qualities that you can make him a great person! And I know my best friend can do it! He will come and your stress will disappear. See yourself. You have become as thin as a broomstick!"

Omkar looked at him. He quickly ran in the hall. Ajinkya chased him. He went left, Ajinkya went right; he jumped from one couch to another, Ajinkya followed him. Finally he caught Omkar.

Ajinkya said, "What? I have become a broomstick!"

He caught Omkar in his arms firm and tickled him.

Omkar laughed and said, "Truth is always truth!"

Ajinkya replied, “Thanks!”

Omkar replied, “Mention me not child!”

Ajinkya laughed. He then gave him a fight. He commented, “Omkar baba!”

February 2004

EIGHT

A week or so went by, but still Ajinkya was unable to take a decision! Many things came into picture when he thought about Kiran. Sometimes his brain supported him, but not his heart; Sometimes his heart did but his brain didn't.

Today the sun had come up early. The first ray of sun suggested that it was going to be a beautiful day. Something special was about to happen. Soon, the employees started moving out of the building.

Ajinkya, Rahul and Krishna followed the mid-shift crowd. They made their way to the tea stall. They halted there and Rahul ordered "Tea and cream roll."

Ajinkya sat on the bench. Ajinkya asked Kiran, "Would you like to come and stay with me in my house? I will take care of your studies!"

Krishna looked at Ajinkya with surprise. Rahul offered a cigarette to Ajinkya.

A smile came on Kiran's face with a couple of doubts.

His mind questioned him, "Why is he showing this generosity and interest in me? Is he going to cheat me? Is he going to use me as Javed is doing right now?"

Ajinkya tapped his shoulder.

"What happened? Where are you lost?"

"But?"

"But what! You want to follow your dreams?"

"Yes. But what about Salim?"

Ajinkya said, "See. I live alone at my flat. So if you want I can give you space in my house!" he took a puff. He continued, "I will help you by all means!"

"But what about Salim?" Kiran inquired.

Ajinkya replied, "Leave it to me! I will speak with him! When does he come here?"

He took a puff of smoke. "He will come at four, tomorrow!"

"Ok I will come tomorrow at four!" Ajinkya said.

Ajinkya looked at the cigarette between his fingers. It had reached its end. He dropped it down. He got up. He smashed it below his sports shoes. He looked at Krishna and Rahul; they had finished their cup of tea and cigarette as well. Ajinkya paid Kiran.

And then, they left.

Nine

The very next day was a normal day for everyone; but was a special day for Kiran!

Ajinkya got ready; dressed in a yellow T-shirt and a pair of jeans. It was three thirty by his wrist watch. He went into the hall. He wore his pair of shoes. And he left to meet Salim.

Ajinkya met Omkar on his way. He was back from school. He had just got down from the school bus. Omkar inquired him, "Where are you going Bhaiya at this time? To the hospital!"

Ajinkya said "I have taken my decision! I am bringing him home! I am going to meet the tea stall owner!"

Omkar smiled and said, "I am happy that you have agreed to take my suggestion! I am proud to be your best friend! But did the owner agree?"

"I am going right now to speak with him!"

"Best of luck!"

"Ok! I will take your leave now!" Ajinkya said.

Omkar nodded. Ajinkya started walking to the main road. He was happy with his decision. There was happiness and light on his face.

He reached the tea stall. He saw Salim sitting on a plastic chair. He was dressed in pathani.

Ajinkya ordered, "one cup of tea!"

Kiran served him a cup of tea. Salim looked at Kiran. Ajinkya sat on the wooden bench. He looked at Salim. He took a sip of the hot syrup. He looked at the vapours. He said, "Hi! You are the owner of this stall?"

Salim replied, "Yes! Why?"

He looked at him. He said "I want to take care of Kiran! I want to take him home!"

Salim looked at him and agitated. He opposed, "Why?"

He replied, "I want him to study! I live alone! I can see a spark in his eyes!"

He cut him off, "No! You can't!"

Ajinkya now lost his temper. He then said, "I will report to the police that you have kept child labourers." Ajinkya strongly added, "But you are making a child work at your place! That's illegal! Are you aware?"

Salim listened to him. He thought for a moment. Still he refused to yield. The sparkling eyes of Salim stared the money. Ajinkya opened his wallet. He looked into it. He removed a note of thousand bucks. He gave him the money. He said, "Every month, I would clear up the losses which would occur due to his absence." Salim kept numb. He agreed.

Kiran smiled. Javed became annoyed with this. The door of a new world was just about to open for Kiran. Ajinkya informed "I will take Kiran home tomorrow afternoon!"

He left. He walked down the street. He went back to work. Kiran went in.

Javed did not want to lose Kiran. It started disturbing him. He walked a couple of steps ahead. He was agitated. "I will be all alone! I will not be able to manage everything!"

Salim said, "No let him go!"

He explained "People can steal! What and where should I keep my eyes! You need to understand!"

Salim looked at the currency in his hand. This world runs on money. Salim got up. He ignored Javed's agitation. He walked to his home. Javed remained all alone.

Kiran was very happy today. Javed chatted with him. Javed knew that by the next dawn their paths would be different. By now Kiran had become an essential part of life.

The Desperate Devil acted on him. The Devil made his way to reach Kiran. Kiran had traveled miles into his dream world! The Devil was ready to pounce on Kiran.

The Devil didn't wish to kill him so easily. He decided to play with him. He held Kiran in his arms. Kiran woke up. Kiran was pulled back from his dream world!

But would Kiran become his prey so easily?

No!

Kiran opened his eyes with a shiver. Kiran battled with the devil. But the devil self replicated and transferred the other into Kiran. Slowly Kiran was pulled into the stream. Finally after within few minutes Kiran gave up. And Kiran was betrayed.

Soon Kiran realized that they were on a wrong way. Kiran pushed back Javed and parted from the devil desire. Kiran displayed protest through his eyes, which ultimately demolished the devil! Finally Kiran safeguarded his innocence.

Kiran walked out. He looked up and saw the bright stars. The 5 degree cold freezed him and the devil. He slowly gained back self-control. The tea stall was parked to his right. He laid down below it. Soon he went deep asleep.

Javed was all alone left in shock. The bedsheets was left wet. Tears ran down his cheeks. He pulled a blanket and he went asleep.

Next morning, Kiran got up with a sigh of hope! He went into the tent and saw Javed still sleeping! He went near him to wake him up but later left him undisturbed. In couple of hours, Kiran would leave for Ajinkya's house and he may not be able to see Javed again! Kiran went closer to kiss Javed's cheek, but he stopped! Kiran walked back, and immediately Javed got up. He did not speak with Kiran. Kiran was pissed off analyzing the silence between them. The last night incidence had given an uneven end to their friendship!

They were back to their routine life. Kiran packed his bag. Kiran turned and looked at Javed but he did not even look back. But they did not speak the entire morning!

By afternoon, Ajinkya arrived at their stall. Kiran saw him. He was happy; but he was also sad! Javed had given him support at the time Kiran was mentally broken! And today, Javed would not even look at him! Time had changed, he turned his nature like the moon changes his phase! Kiran went in. He lifted his bag! He eagerly waited for Javed to say a few words to him!

'If he asks me to stay back, I will but I want him to speak with me!'

So he walked slowly. He did not turn to have a glance of Javed. Ajinkya lifted the bag in his hand. He walked and Kiran followed him. He left, but Javed did not say anything. He did not even look at him. Kiran's ears were eager to hear Javed's voice.

But the silence waved off this relation!

Soon Ajinkya and Kiran reached this society! Kiran looked at the society name plate, Nilima Housing Society. He glanced at the greenery in the society compound; it filled his mind with peace!

They climbed up the stairs to reach home. Ajinkya knocked on the door. Omkar opened it. He saw Ajinkya and Kiran, and he gave a smile. Ajinkya smiled; but Kiran was not in state to smile. He had to struggle to hide the tsunami in his mind!

Rahul's family was eagerly waiting at the door. They greeted them. Rahul's mother tapped Ajinkya's shoulder in appreciation for his decision. He smiled at Omkar. He thanked Omkar for his support. Everyone was happily smiling, but Kiran remained pale and nervous.

Kiran murmured, "I have realized one thing that Javed is selfish! He just wanted to have me! He wanted to fulfill his greed. Javed did not even speak a word with me today since morning, just because he got denied! I am starting a new journey to fulfill my dreams, Javed should have been happy! But no, he is selfish! Each day began with a kiss and ended with the same! I hate him! My trust is broken; don't know if I will be able to trust anyone in this world!"

As Kiran entered the flat, Ajinkya asked Omkar to take his bag in.

Rahul's mother noticed Ajinkya's tension. She replied, "Don't worry! This place is new; Kiran might need time to open up with us!"

He replied, "Hmm!"

Omkar picked up the bag and went in. He glanced at Kiran from a distance!

Kiran was numb for a few days. He spoke little; he was confused with his own things and thoughts. Then slowly, Kiran started speaking with Omkar. But Kiran lived with a feeling of guilt and he was unable to speak about it. He fell short of words, whenever tired to speak anything! He started fumbling! Soon Kiran preferred being alone, away from friends; but still Omkar did not leave Kiran alone! And slowly they became good friends. Slowly as time passed, their bonding became strong!

TEN

It was six in the evening. The sun has settled on the left. On the right, a bright half moon ascended the sky.

Ajinkya had gone to the hospital. Kiran was alone in the house; and Omkar had just finished his home work. He was in his house.

He was wearing red shorts and sitting on the couch bare-chest. He was watching a comedy show on the Television.

The society children climbed the stairs to call him. When he heard a knock at the door, he opened it. He said happily, "Hey hi friends!"

They could hear the comedian speaking on the show, a cooker whistling and Omkar's mother calling him.

Mother said, "Omkar who is it?"

Omkar looked back and replied, "My friends!" He looked at Yash and continued, "Yes you were saying something?"

Yash said "Yes I said! We were waiting for you down since when! Finally we have come to take you along with us!"

Omkar looked back again. He said, "Ma, I am going down!"

Abhishek said, "Hey wear a shirt first!"

He replied, "Yes! I am coming!"

He went into his room. Yash stepped into the house. One by one everyone walked in. Some of his friends sat on the couch! They giggled at the acts performed by the comedians on the show.

Omkar wore a yellow T-shirt and came from his room. He said "I am ready! Let's move!"

He wore his brown sandals standing at the door. She said, "Omkar, no fighting OK!" He switched off the television.

He replied "Yes mom!"

She said, "And take care!"

"Uff! She has again started her lecture Run!" He pulled the door. The automatic lock closed. He ran downstairs with his friends.

They reached the car parking. Omkar inquired, "So what to play?"

Sonu said, "Let's play hide and seek!"

Everyone said, "Ya let's play hide and seek!"

Suddenly, Omkar came up with an idea. He said to his friends, "Let's call Kiran to play with us!"

Sonu said, "Fine!"

They all rushed up. Yash said, "Let's have a race! Let's see who reaches first!"

Some climbed the stairs; a few went by the lift. They reached the second floor.

They showed thumbs down. Pranav said, "Its fine! The lift was not available!"

Omkar rang the bell once and, then for the second time! Sonu and Yash took a deep breath as the kids coming by lift reached. Kiran opened the door. He questioned with a surprise "Omkar what happened? Need water?"

He replied, "No! We have come here to call you down to play with us!"

Kiran said, "I cannot!"

"Why?"

"I am not feeling good!"

Short, eight year old Pratik with a small face, said, "You're alone in the house, so you will not feel good! Come with us!"

Yash, who lived next door said, "Come on! We will play hide and seek. We will love to make you our friend!"

Kiran protested, "I don't want to come down and play with you all."

Omkar asked with anger, "What's the problem?"

"I said no, means no!" and Kiran banged the door on their face.

Everyone felt insulted. They looked at Omkar with anger. They went down slowly; none even spoke a word with Omkar! They crawled down with sad faces. They reached the parking. They sat on the bench quietly. Everyone's mood was spoiled, because of Kiran's behaviour!

They murmured; Omkar was standing silently next to them, with his head down. Slowly one by one everyone left. Omkar also went back to home.

He felt insulted in front of his friends for the first time; but since he never kept anything in his mind, he forgot this insult, when he sat in front of the television.

ELEVEN

It was 5 PM, Tuesday. Omkar had finished his studies for the day. He walked down to meet his best friend. He climbed the stairs of Nilima Society. He knocked at Ajinkya's door. Ajinkya opened the door.

He said, "Hey hi Omkar! Come in!"

He moved in. He closed the door and sat on the couch. Ajinkya went in. Omkar switched on the television set. He looked at Omkar and said, "Omkar, Kiran is sleeping! Take care of him! I am going to work!"

Omkar went in the bedroom to see Kiran. He entered the bedroom. A silent track was running on the radio. Kiran was sleeping on the bed, covered with a blanket. The window next to the bed was partially open. A breeze was blowing into the room. Kiran was sleeping in peace. He sat next to Kiran. He murmured, "Kiran looks good! But I don't know why he gets angry about each and everything? His behaviour is odd!"

Suddenly Omkar saw a bag. He murmured, "I don't think this bag belongs to Ajinkya!"

He got up slowly. The alarm system in Omkar's mind buzzed loud! He said "What's there in it?"

With silent steps, he reached the bag kept in the corner on the stool near Kiran's head. He reached the bag.

RJ Subodh announced, "Next track for you from Kuch Kuch Hota Hain, Enjoy it Punekars!"

He opened the bag. He murmured "Let's see! What is there?"

He saw some documents and photos kept in it. He removed them. He looked at those documents. He found Kiran's 3rd standard school identity-card, where Kiran was dressed in girl's uniform and had plaits. And he also found a certificate in his bag. The documents gave him 440 volts shock!

He murmured, "I need to tell this to Ajinkya! This is shocking! I need to tell him the truth!"

He walked to the window. Then he thought, "But there might be some problem, because of which Kiran is hiding this thing! If I tell this to Ajinkya, it might create a misunderstanding between him and Kiran!"

He remained numb for a minute. Later he concluded, "Let the right time come! Till the time I will investigate into this!"

He looked at the documents again. He went back and kept the documents at its place. He went down to the parking. He looked towards Ajinkya who was busy wiping the dusted collected on his bike.

He inquired, "Bhaiya sometimes Kiran behaves like an alien! What's wrong with Kiran?

Ajinkya replied, The place and people around are new for him! So he maybe feeling odd man out! Let's give him time and soon I hope he will be fine dude!

"What do you mean bhaiya?" he inquired.

Ajinkya looked at Omkar and said,

"You always asked na! Why do I live alone in this big house?"

Omkar nodded his head and said, "Hmm!"

"I will narrate my own life story to you both!"

"Fine! OK!" Omkar caught Ajinkya's right arm. He dragged him and said, "Let's begin!"

Ajinkya requested him, "Not today yaar! Please!"

Omkar nodded by his head sideways and said, "Tell the story today."

They went upstairs to Ajinkya's house. Omkar opened the door. Ajinkya was still pleading, "Not today man!"

Omkar pushed Ajinkya in front. Omkar sat on the couch. Ajinkya stood tense. He was wondering what to say. And from where should to start?

Ajinkya rubbed Omkar's head with his palms. Omkar glanced at him. Ajinkya blushed. He said, "Don't stare! I am feeling nervous!"

Kiran was sleeping in the bedroom. He heard them speaking. Ajinkya went to washroom. Omkar followed him there. Ajinkya went in. he looked back. He saw Omkar standing behind at the entrance of washroom.

"Hey where are you coming with me?"

"I know you're trying to avoid the topic! Want to wash your face? Wash, wash!"

He came in and shut the door. Ajinkya stood in front of the wash basin. He looked in the mirror. He looked at his reflection. His eyes were red. There were artistic curve lines on his forehead. He was stressed. He never shared his problems with Omkar, his best Friend. But today, he had to! And that would make Kiran comfortable.

He bent down to wash his face. He turned the tap on. Omkar looked at him. Ajinkya avoided him. He got his hand in front and filled water in his palm. He looked up at the mirror. He splashed water on his face. He tried to wash away his stress.

He splashed water on his face twice and thrice. But stress was not ready to leave him. He rubbed his face with his palms. He felt better. He turned off the tap. Omkar pulled the small pink towel from the rod next to him. He gave it to Ajinkya. Ajinkya wiped his face with it. He felt fresh. He looked at Omkar. He gave the towel to Omkar. But Omkar didn't take it.

Omkar said with an attitude "God has given you hands! Keep it yourself!"

Ajinkya blushed. He threw the towel down and caught Omkar in his arms. Omkar smiled. Ajinkya tickled at his waist. He started laughing and said, "Leave me! Leave me!" He sat on the floor.

Kiran had a frightening nightmare. His heart also said, "Leave me! Leave me!" he started changing his sleeping position from left to right, right to left! His eyes were closed. Stress line started appearing on his face.

The Tom and Jerry fight continued in the washroom. Ajinkya said, “Now you move out! I have to pee!”

He pulled his hand and tried to push him to the door. But he did not move. He said, “That’s good! I too want to empty my tank!”

“What?”

“I will not leave you alone!”

“OK!”

They both emptied their bladders and moved out of the washroom.

Ajinkya went into the kitchen. He prepared masala tea. Omkar went to the bedroom. Kiran was sitting on the bed. He had a blanket over him. He had just got up. He was wearing a white shirt and white pant with big black dots on it. He rubbed his eyes with his palm. His face revealed his tension. Omkar greeted him, “Good morning Kiran!”.

Kiran replied with a smile, “Good morning Omkar!”

Omkar asked, “How are you?”

Kiran kept silent. He changed the topic. He asked, “Where is Ajinkya bhaiya?”

“He is in the kitchen.”

"Oops! I am late! It's 10:30."

"That's fine! Today is Sunday."

Kiran got up in hurry. He went in the washroom attached to the bedroom. Omkar followed him there. Kiran looked at Omkar.

"Hey be out!"

Kiran pushed him out. He locked the door. Omkar's doubt became strong. He went in the hall. He saw Ajinkya sitting on the couch. Omkar sat beside him.

Time passed by, but Ajinkya couldn't dare to begin narrating his life story. Omkar saw that Ajinkya was not feeling comfortable so he too didn't bring up the topic again.

TWELVE

It's four o'clock. Today, the sun rays are not burning the skin. Today, they are just enlightening the world. There is a cool breeze flowing all around.

Ajinkya woke up early and a bath early. He moved out of the washroom. He had kept his clothes on the bed. Ajinkya stood in front of the dressing table mirror. He wore a blue shirt and a formal pleat less black pant. He combed his hair.

Kiran was in the hall. He was busy watching a quiz show on a Television channel.

He went in the kitchen. He packed his Tiffin. He kept the food for Kiran's lunch properly in the fridge. He kept the milk to boil. He went in the hall. He saw Kiran staring the

T. V. set and writing something on the paper. He was busy counting something of his fingers.

Ajinkya went to the balcony. He saw Omkar. Omkar just stepped down from his school-bus. He walked into his apartment.

Ajinkya went back in the kitchen. He poured milk in two glasses. He picked the glasses and went in the hall. He kept the glasses on the centre-table. He went to Kiran. He was still busy in writing.

Ajinkya looked on to the page, He was eager to know what Kiran was upto. Kiran wrote something and then scribbled it and started writing at a different part of the page. The whole page was decorated in the same fashion.

Ajinkya could only understand some letters. Those letters were on the right: a, r, i, a; letters at the left: a, e, i, c, a.

He eagerly inquired, "Kiran what are you trying to write?"

Kiran didn't look up at Ajinkya. He said, "The question is, what are the common factors in names of these continents?"

Kiran reacted "But where are the continents?"

He then recognized what Kiran had written.

The word at right formed, Africa and at the left, America.

Ajinkya thought for a moment. He scratched his head. He got the answer. He smiled. He said, “It’s very simple!”

Kiran looked up at him. He had a question-mark on his face. He asked, “How?”

Ajinkya answered, “Each continent begins and ends with the same vowels. Check it!”

Omkar looked down on his page. He found that Ajinkya was correct. He looked at Ajinkya and smiled. Ajinkya picked up the glass and came to Kiran. He said, “Here is your milk.”

“Ok!”

He took the glass from Ajinkya’s hand. He drank the milk and kept the glass on the table.

“I have kept your food in the fridge. Eat it on time.”

“Ok!”

Ajinkya drank the milk from his glass in one sip. He kept the glass on the table. He sat on the chair near the footwear shelf. He removed a pair of black socks and black shoes. He wore them. He took the tiffin and went.

Almost ten minutes later, Kiran went in the kitchen and washed the glasses and kept them at their respective places.

He went in the bedroom. He picked his bag. He opened it. He searched something in his bag. He found some coins. He grabbed them. He kept them in his pocket. He went into the hall. He switched off the T.V. He wore his sandals and took the door keys. He locked the door and went down. He walked towards the street. Omkar noticed Kiran from his gallery

Kiran came back in ten minutes. He walked very quietly looking here and there, like a criminal.

Omkar noticed this odd behaviour of his. The alarm in his mind rang. It rang loudly. The inspector in him woke up. He recalled. Ajinkya had told him not to leave Kiran alone.

The inspector said, "Omkar something is wrong! Let's go!"

He brought his hands together and interlocked them. It appeared like a pistol.

The inspector continued, "He walked like a criminal! Hope everything is fine!"

He went in the hall. He wore his slippers and went down the stairs. He went into Ajinkya's apartment. He climbed the stairs very carefully. He walked like a cat with no noise. He walked exactly like 007 James Bond.

He reached Ajinkya's house. He bent towards the door. The door was closed. He put his ears on the door.

There was a pin-drop silence in the room. Omkar rang the bell. But he didn't get any response from inside. Suddenly he heard a bang. It seemed like the window was pushed outward and it had banged against the outer wall. He heard footsteps approaching the door. He heard the sound of the fan turned on. There was someone standing at the door. But still there was no reply no response from inside.

Omkar rang the bell continuously twice, thrice. The inspector murmured, 'Darwaza todh do Daya!' Suddenly the sound of the fan stopped. And Kiran opened the door with a smile. Omkar stepped in. He took air in. Something was burning. He looked up. The fan had almost stopped. He looked at the open windows. 'May be one of these window banged' the inspector inspected. Inspector continued, 'Can't say! Maybe Kiran was smoking! Need evidence to confirm that! But I doubt about it! Kuch toh gadbad hai Daya!'

Kiran stammered and said, "Omkar relax! Have a seat!"

Omkar sat on the couch. Kiran sat next to him. Kiran was chewing something. "It smelling good", Inspector said, "Divert Kiran! Only then we can investigate!"

"Ok!", Omkar calm the inspector.

"Kiran bring me a glass of water!"

Kiran got up. He went in the kitchen. Omkar looked around.

The inspector, "Chalo sab kam pe lag jao, aur ghar ka kona kona chan maro! (Get back to work guys. Search each and every corner)"

Omkar looked around the couch. He noticed a butt which was still burning partially. He snapped. "So I am correct!"

He thought for a moment. Kiran came back. He gave him a glass of water. He drank it.

He said to himself, "Now I cannot leave Kiran alone anytime!"

He returned the empty glass.

Omkar pretended to be normal and unaware about Kiran's act. He said, "Let's play something!"

"What?"

Omkar thought for a moment. He said, "Let's play carrom!"

Omkar went in. He looked for the carrom-board. He went in the study room. He removed the standing carrom facing the wall. He looked for coins. He removed the coins. He went in the hall. He asked Kiran to help him. They both came in. Omkar picked the carrom-board and asked Kiran to carry the coins and the powder out.

He kept the carrom-board in the hall. He wiped the board with a cloth. Then he kept it on the floor. He sat on one side of the carrom. He took the powder and spread it over the board. Kiran sat right opposite to Omkar. He piled the coins as per colour. There stood two tower one brown and the other black standing next to each other and had a common top-floor. It was pink in colour.

Omkar gave the striker to Kiran to start the game.

THIRTEEN

Who is Pooja?

Ajinkya walked down the street to the doctor's clinic. He knocked the door. Dr. Pooja is busy writing something on a scribbling pad. She said, "Come in". Ajinkya came in. He stood at the door.

Dr. Pooja had loved Ajinkya since school times. They both were in the same class, same division. Pooja never tried to open up and tell him that she loved him. She was a shy girl. God has again brought them in front of each other. But did Ajinkya remember her? She has changed; her bob-cut hair, today reaches her stomach. Her round potato face has grown long. But even today she is as simple as she was earlier. She is lost in her past.

Ajinkya knocked at the door again. The sound broke her link. She looked at him. She said, "Come in!"

Ajinkya came in. She stared him. He asked, "Dr. Pooja child specialist?"

She realized that he has yet not recognized her. She was disappointed.

She said with a professional attitude, "Yes! How may I help you?"

He came ahead. She said, "Have a seat!"

Ajinkya pulled the chair back. He sat on the chair. She looked down and continued writing.

Ajinkya said, "My name is Ajinkya Jadhav! I need your help!"

She dropped the pen. She ran her eyes on his face. But she avoided eye contact with Ajinkya. She inquired, "What type of help do you want from me?"

"Well, I live at a distance of five minutes from here! I have a child living with me, who is always quiet. I feel that something is eating him from within. I don't know what to do? I need your help!"

She looked up at his face. She said, "Some children are quiet by nature! How can you say that something is wrong?"

Ajinkya took a deep breath. He said, "I have lost my family. I live alone. So I decided to help someone who is really in need! Kiran is a ten - eleven year old kid. He was a child labourer. He has no family. He wants to become a good person in life! So I decided to take his responsibility!"

She kept quiet. The words had stuck in his throat. She looked at him with love. She liked his initiative for Kiran. She started falling in love with him again.

He gathered his words. He continued, "I brought him home. But since then he has become very quiet. He does not speak much. He does not play. He always likes to be in the house. What should I do to make him happy?"

Dr. Pooja looked down on the prescription pad. She thought for a moment.

She looked up and inquired, "When did you bring him home?"

Ajinkya replied, "Almost a week ago!"

"Was he the same in nature earlier?""

Ajinkya replied firmly, "No!"

"Hmm!" She thought for a moment. She said, "I need to check him!"

"So should I bring him in the evening or tomorrow morning?"

"No! If you bring him here, he would pretend to be normal!"

"Then?"

"I will come to your house as a stranger!"

"That's fine!" Ajinkya smiled. He said, "Give me a piece of paper! I will give you my address!"

He stretched his hand to take a pen from the pen stand.

"Do you still live, where you lived six years ago?"

"Yes!? But how do you know about it?"

"Ajinkya, I am Pooja Joshi!"

Ajinkya ran a search report in his memory but he couldn't remember anyone by that name.

She said, "You studied in Camp Education right?"

"Yes!"

"I was your classmate from first to tenth standard!"

Ajinkya still couldn't remember her. The reason behind this might be that his brain was still occupied with Kiran and only Kiran. He behaved as if he remembered her. He looked at her with surprise, as if two best friends have met a decade later. He did not want to hurt her by not recognising her!

"Ok! So done you are coming to my house tomorrow!"

"Yes! Tomorrow evening at five!"

"Ok!"

Ajinkya got up. He shook hand with her and smiled. He turned towards the door and walked ahead. He stopped at the door and looked back. He was unable to remember who Pooja was! He left. He looked at the name plate at the entrance of the clinic.

Dr. Pooja Joshi MBBS (Mumbai) Child Specialist

Still the name didn't rang a bell in Ajinkya's mind; but by now surely it had given him a severe headache! He said, "Forget it! Let's go home! Kiran is alone!"

FOURTEEN

Dr. Pooja went to Ajinkya's house. She was visiting the place after many years.

She said to herself, "I still remember the last time I went to his house; it was on his 12th birthday party. I remember he came in civil dress to the school. During the First Period, we sang the birthday jingle for him!"

"I had started sweating when he approached my desk. I had stammered and said," So when is the birthday party?' He had replied, 'Come to my house this evening.' And that evening I had went to his place last! Today while walking towards Ajinkya's house I am scared."

She took a long breath and continued, "During school days, I was unaware that I loved him! After the 10th Board exams, everyone went their own way. We got separated as well. And that's when I realized that I loved him. But by then we both had lost contact. I did not have hopes meeting him. I tried to go to his house couple of times, but couldn't make it! Many questions popped up like what I would say when I went there..."

She stopped. She took a breath and sat on the wooden bench before Ajinkya's apartment building.

She got up and walked towards Ajinkya's house.

For Ajinkya, Pooja was always a good friend. Today she is not only his friend, but a Doctor as well. True, limitations and gaps had erupted between them. She climbed the stairs slowly. She rang the door bell. A bird sang. Ajinkya walked towards the door. He looked through the magic eye. He found Dr. Pooja at the door. He was happy seeing her.

He said with a smile, "Welcome Pooja!"

She smiled and said, "Hi!"

He said, "Come in!"

She walked in.

Ajinkya said, "Thank you for taking out some time on my request!"

She replied, "That's fine!"

She looked around. She saw Omkar sitting on the couch. He was busy scribbling something on the newspaper with a ball point pen. Ajinkya requested her, "Have a seat!"

She replied, "Yes! Thanks!"

She sat on the couch. She kept her purse to her right. Ajinkya went in. She said, "Hi!" Omkar looked up and glanced at her. He said, "Hi!"

He looked in the newspaper and continued colouring the cartoons printed on the page. She looked in the newspaper. She said, "What is your name?"

"Omkar!" he replied.

She scanned the room but couldn't find anyone else. Ajinkya brought a glass of water from kitchen. He said, "This is Omkar, my best friend!"

She replied "OK!"

She took a sip of water. She looked at Ajinkya. Ajinkya took her to the study room. The curtains were closed. The lights were on. Kiran was sitting with a bunch of full size story-books. She was sitting on a steel chair. A soft music could be heard in the background.

Ajinkya said, "Kiran!"

Kiran looked at Ajinkya. He then looked at Pooja. Ajinkya said, "This is Pooja! She was my classmate!"

She looked at Ajinkya.

She said to herself, "He remembers me! May be, he loves me!" She smiled and said, "He introduced me as a friend and not as child specialist and not even as Doctor. He loves me!"

Kiran smiled and said, "Hi!"

Pooja replied, "Hi! Can I sit with you?"

Kiran said, "Sure!"

She sat on the plastic chair. Ajinkya pulled a chair kept in the corner. He sat on it. Kiran continued reading the story book. Pooja interrupted Kiran twice, but he didn't speak much. So she peeped in the story book.

She said, "So what type of story-books do you like?"

He counter-attacked her, "I?"

She looked around and said, "I hope only you are reading a story book! Right?"

He looked up and said, "Yes!"

He looked at Pooja. He thought for a moment and said, "I like story-books, like, like Cindrella, and Tinkle!"

"I too like to read story-books!"

Kiran gave a strange look. She inquired, "Why? Only kids can read it, is it so?"

"No!"

"Then let me see!"

Kiran gave the book to Pooja; and this moment sealed their friendship.

Soon, Pooja and Kiran became good friends. They gossiped together and had snacks together. The clock indicated that it was getting rather late for Pooja. Ajinkya left to go to the hospital.

She looked back at Ajinkya. She opened her mouth to say something to Ajinkya but the words halted on her tongue. She asked Omkar about Ajinkya.

He replied that Ajinkya went to the hospital on daily basis. She doubted that something has happened of which she was not aware. She moved out of the study room. She saw Omkar playing video game on the television. Omkar meanwhile sensed that something was brewing in Pooja. He saw a different shine in Pooja's eyes.

FIFTEEN

The next day, Ajinkya went down the street to Pooja's clinic. The birds were singing morning hymns. Dr. Pooja was sitting on her chair holding a pen in her hand. She was busy writing the case study of Kiran on a rough paper. She had found out some observations, on the basis of which, she had drawn a conclusion. She read the conclusion, "Kiran is haunted by his past and has not yet spoken much because he has yet not established trust in Ajinkya!"

She exclaimed, "That's shocking! Kiran has yet not established trust in Ajinkya? Something has happened in his past which is bothering him!"

Ajinkya knocked at the door. She looked up and says, "Come in!"

Ajinkya went in. She got up and greeted, "hi! Ajinkya how are you?"

"I am fine!" He sat on the chair. "Did you study anything about Kiran?"

"Yes!" She sat on her chair slowly.

"So! What do we need to do?"

She said, "I think, there is something which is bothering him from within! There has something happened in his past which is disturbing him!"

"So what should be our next step?"

She said to herself, "This is the best time! Let's play a game!"

She said to Ajinkya, "You can take him on an outing!"

Ajinkya replied, "Ok!"

She hesitated to talk. She gathered some courage and said, "The way to make him comfortable is to remove the thing which is bothering him!"

Ajinkya questioned, "How?"

"Well! Does he know about your past?"

"No!"

"Tell him everything about your past! Soon you will see its effects!"

She took a deep breath. Ajinkya refreshed his past.

"I need sometime! I need to study Kiran!"

Ajinkya questioned, "Are you sure, it will work?"

"Yes it will!" she smiled.

Ajinkya got up.

"I need to go! I have some work!" Ajinkya said.

He held her hand. He turned and walked towards the door.

She said, "Ajinkya!"

He looked back and said, "Yes?"

"And one more thing!" She got up from her seat. She picked up a visiting card. She went and stood in front of Ajinkya.

She said, "I need to advice you on one thing! Apply for adoption to avoid difficulties in near future!"

She gave him the visiting card. He read the card. She continued, "I will visit your house every two or three days."

He removed his wallet and kept the card in. He removed some cash and gave her the fees.

She visited his house on regular basis. Omkar was now pretty sure that there was something brewing vigorously in Pooja. Was she in love with Ajinkya? But she always visited when Ajinkya was not there at home in the evening time. She quite often inquired about Ajinkya.

SIXTEEN

Today is the first Saturday of the month. Ajinkya has a weekly off. And Omkar has a holiday as well.

Usually on a holiday he has to go to the hospital in the night. But today due to some reason he will not go. And he will sleep in the night.

Ajinkya got up early around eight. Kiran was asleep. He had tea and then went for a shower.

He was stressed with his busy schedule of the whole week: 10pm to 6am at work; and noon to 7pm in the hospital.

The cold water falling on his head from the shower took away his tiredness. His disturbed mind became calm. The negative thoughts peeled off like the dirt from his skin. He felt good when he came out.

He saw Kiran awake. He was folding the blanket he had taken in the night. He wore a white half shirt and a night pant. He had combed his hair well. Kiran went to take a shower.

Ajinkya came into the hall. He saw Omkar sitting on the couch. The newspaper was lying on the table. A small plate was lying on it, right in front of Omkar. Maybe he had some cookies. The food particles on the plate and around his lips matched.

Ajinkya said, "Hey Omkar, how are you?"

Omkar replied, "As usual! Ask something different man."

Ajinkya thought for a moment. He then said, "Ate cookies ha! You should keep the plate back in its place!"

"Usually you do this work Right!"" Omkar paused. He looked at Ajinkya. He said, "It's always a waiter's work."

Ajinkya reacted "What? Are you trying to say, I am a waiter?"

Omkar replied in a meek voice, "Just kidding!" Ajinkya sat on the couch. Ajinkya raised his arm to grab the newspaper. Omkar instantly picked it up. He opened it and acted as if he was reading the news. Ajinkya switched on the Television set. He surfed many channels with the remote. Omkar threw the paper on his chest. He quickly pulled the remote from Ajinkya's hand.

Ajinkya was now frustrated by Omkar's behaviour. He said, "You're just too much!" He replied again with a humble voice, "Yes I am!"

An hour had past. Kiran was still in the shower. He was sitting under the running shower. He was still wearing yesterday's clothes. He was lost in his thoughts.

"Should I tell the truth to Ajinkya?" His mind responded, "No! Are you mad! He will throw you out! Don't show your foolishness here."

"But that's absolutely wrong!" "So what! Do you want to repeat your past again?"

"No, I don't!"

"So keep quiet! And now get up and move out" commanded his mind.

He got up. He turned off the shower. He stripped off his clothes. He dropped them down. He soaked his clothes in soap water.

He sat down. He had the same conversation with his mind. He tried hard to convince his mind, but couldn't. Sometime later he felt cold. He then realized that he was sitting on the floor. He got up and washed the clothes; he wore clean clothes.

Omkar was watching his favourite cartoon Supandi. Ajinkya had finished reading the newspaper. Omkar said, "Bhaiya! It's almost an hour and half, Kiran has been in the shower. What is he doing?"

He blushed. Ajinkya glanced at him and inquired, "What is he doing?"

He replied "That's what I am asking you!"

"Hey!" Ajinkya got up. He walked to Omkar. "I know, what you're thinking! You..!" He tickled him at his neck. Kiran came out with washed clothes in his hand; he looked at them. They were sitting in pin drop silence in the room. Ajinkya walked out of the house.

SEVENTEEN

In Search of The Past

Omkar went into the study room. Kiran dressed up. He looked for Omkar. He saw Omkar searching for something. He had moved all the books from their place. The study room now looked like a secondhand book stall. Books piled up like pillars.

Kiran walked to Omkar. He said, "Omkar what are you looking for?"

He did not reply. He inquired again, "Should I help you?"

He replied, "Do you know where Ajinkya's Personal Diary is?"

"Yes!"

"Where is it kept?"

"In the first drawer! There!"

Kiran pointed to the computer table. Omkar dropped the books which he was carrying in his hand. He opened the drawer. Kiran picked the books lying on the floor.

Kiran questioned, "But why do you want it?"

"Be quiet!"

He found the brown leather covered diary. The year mentioned on the front cover in golden was '2004'! He picked it up and took it to the hall. Kiran arranged the books to one side.

He wondered, "What is he looking for? I want to see! Let's go!"

He saw Omkar sitting on the couch. He sat on the left arm of the couch. Omkar kept the dairy on his lap. He opened it.

EIGHTEEN

Executive Diary

I am Ajinkya Jadhav. There are many memories with this house. I spent my childhood here. My father gifted this flat to my mom on their third marriage anniversary! In those days, a family that owned a one bedroom hall kitchen was entitled as middle class family!

There were many pictures kept in the diary. One of them was when Ajinkya when he was ten and he was quiet healthy. He was accompanied by his young parents in various postures. His father was a Marathi theatre artist, a few pictures of the plays as well! Another picture of Ajinkya and Neha with smileys around! Both holding each other's hands and had a background of a beach!

I passed my 12th standard exam like every average student does, and I got admission in a college nearby. It was just ten minutes walking distance from place!

I was a part of a class whose strength was almost 100. The building was well maintained and was surrounded by a semicircular garden. Basketball ground was at the front and football ground at the backside!

I was crazy about football. I used to go to the college wearing studs. And I was ever ready for football. And our college ground was big enough to conduct three football matches at the same time!

There was dense forest surrounding the ground on three sides. The ground was fenced from all sides. The goal posts always had nets tied. So we played football for long hours. Our bags were kept below the tree at the entrance of the ground!

Our professors were good! They never raised voice, unless we bunked lectures daily! Because we had won Pune Zonal football championship twice!

I was in my final year of B. Com. when I met her!

I remember that day!

Due to major change in syllabus, a meeting was conducted and so the college decided to give a common-off for the entire day! We were happy about it. That day, we played football from the very first hour of the college. And none of us had any plans to go back home!

Couples were sitting under the tamarind tree. I went to the ground along with my friends.

Some Girls were sitting under the trees planted near the fence inside the ground. Majority of them were busy gossiping about movies and few were completing notes. Well, movies were one of the topic of their gossip, what I could hear!

Some of them were playing antakshri. But there were some who became our audience and cheered our game!

Our match began. We distributed ourselves in teams. I stood as captain of one team and my friend Arun as captain of the opposite team.

The match began. I played as a forward player. We made our heavy weight friend Humpty Dumpty a goal keeper. I didn't knew his real name. They scored two goals back-to-back. And that was heights, heights means heights!

But in next ten minutes, everything was under-control! And we equaled the match, thanks to the goal scored by me!

The burning hot sun tortured us, but we didn't stop playing! The sweat ran down our necks.

Suddenly, one of us flicked the football. It flew in the air and dashed on the trunk of the tree where the girls were sitting.

We went running to collect the ball. The angry cats looked us! I quietly took the ball.

I saw a girl who was sitting right in the middle of all of her friends. But was busy completing notes that too, for one of her friend! That impressed me!

I instantly got attracted to her. I was lost in her. Slowly, unknowingly I moved towards her. She saw a shadow approaching her. She instantly looked up. Her beautiful black eyes was like the whirl and I lost my way in it!. Soon my ears heard a name whispered by her friends, 'Neha!

And she looked back.

I looked at her more attentively. She was fair and very beautiful, with a well-chiseled face and features. She had a plait which reached till her waist. She looked healthy which added to her attractiveness. She looked at me and smiled. Her smile made me more crazy. Her eyebrows were a beautiful black. Her red lips looked superb!

She was dressed in a black half Sleeve T-shirt and a blue jeans pant. Her sandals were kept to her left.

Oh no! Just when I was deeply studying her, I heard my teammates calling me. I avoided them for a while but then all of my friends started shouting out my name. That's when she came to know my name. And it spoiled my romantic mood and my concentration as well! And now to keep their mouth

I had to go back to play! My friends laughed and made my fun. They started inquiring about her. But I ignored it.

The game continued for almost another hour. And after that we were tired. We ended the game three-two. We had won the match! Wow!! Hip hip Hurray!

We started walking towards the other side of the ground. We sat under the shelter of the tree. We spread down on the green grass. It was cold! We got relief from the heat!

Constantly, I could see her face. I was mentally there around her! She was speaking with her friends there far away from us. But I could hear her speaking.

Ten days passed by. I had become restless without seeing her. It took me ten days to acknowledge that I was in love with her!

Finally the day came when I went to speak with Neha. The girls who were chit-chatting in the background became more keen to listen to our talks. Only I and Neha were audible! Her heartbeats increased and mine as well! It was pretty loud! I could hear a romantic song on someone's mobile phone!

Him dil De chuke sanam, tere ho gaye hai him Teri kasam...

She tried to ignore me for some time and continued writing. Then suddenly I don't know what happened... I went on my knees. She stopped writing. She looked at me. I closed her book. I picked it from her lap, kept it to one side. I went close to her face, very close.... I looked in her eyes. She looked in my eyes. We sensed mutual, instant love for each other. She smiled.

She looked at my face. And a cold breeze ran on my whole body.

I said, "Hello! Neha. How are you?"

Everyone around her may be knew the reason why I had come there!

She replied with a smile, "Fine!"

A girl looked up. She made faces and commented, "'How boring!" She got back to complete her project.

"Neha!"" I said in a low voice, ""A...Neha, I love you!"

Everyone looked at us.

"Do you like me Neha?"

She looked at me and she twinkled her eyes with joy. She had accepted my love. And I, I was on the seventh heaven of happiness! Everyone got up smiling and clapped for us.

Earlier to bunk lectures, football practice was my reason; but now I had another one, I was in love! I had to give some time to Neha! For us, three hours was like fifteen minutes. For us, the whole day meant something!

We left our house on time. My mother and father were shocked. Their lazy son got up on time, rather before everyone; got well dressed! I started keeping a small comb in my pocket. I took care of my hair and my looks and every single thing!

For sure, there was something wrong, they felt!

Neha rode her cycle to reach the college. I walked down the street with my friends. She would daily pass by me, since my rascal friends were with me, I couldn't look at her. Few days later she fixed a handle mirror to her right. And we looked at each other the mirror! She is intelligent!

I kept my college bag at the entrance. We had a friend named Harish Gupta. It was his work to bring the football. He used to carry it daily to the college.

One day, his mother asked him, "You never played football since childhood! Do you play football in the college?"

"Yes! Without me no one can play football! I have the most important role in the game!" he replied.

His father asked "What's that?" He folded his hands and looked at him. His mother wrapped the pallu of her saree in.

He answered, "I am the Referee!"

His father replied with shock, "What?"

His parents looked at each other. His mother didn't knew what a referee was. But from her husband's reaction she guessed that her son does something that is crap! She went in the kitchen with anger!

She came out. She threw utensils on him. His father was enjoying the show. He didn't want to interfere or else he would be smashed in between them.

That day he was late! We were frustrated sitting and just sitting. I was feeling bored. And we were missing our game. I was missing Neha.

She had went to attend a very important lecture. The lecture was conducted on a different floor. She was sitting next to the window. He came. We ignored him. We were sitting under the tree at the entrance of the ground. We behaved like a stranger. He sat in between us. He opened his mouth to say something. Then and there, I slapped him. And everyone was startled. He shouted. We stopped. Then he told us about this incident. We caught our stomach and laughed like crazy. We rolled on the mud. Neha looked down from the window. She messaged me. The message popped up in my mobile. I read it. And after that I couldn't dare to laugh.

"What's wrong? Everyone is looking down."

We didn't dare to look up. But I messaged the incident to her. She laughed. The professor asked her to walk out. She left.

I remember that day. Neha wound up her work from the library. She came at the entrance. She sat under the tree. She picked up my bag and kept it on her lap. She waited for me daily and this was her routine, everyday. And I used to make her wait daily. I always pretended that I didn't see her.

In my bag, there was a calculator which I never used; a compass-box in which there were pens gifted by Neha, but the ink had dried up. There was an Accounts book and an extra book and a deodorant and yes a water bottle!

Sometime later, I approached her. I walked slowly like a hero of some cinema. Sweat ran on my neck. My T-shirt was wet. She looked at me and gave me a smile. I reached out to her; but the foul odour of my sweat reached her before me.

She caught her nose tight. She made weird expressions on her face. She was unable to breathe. She didn't like the odour, but still she welcomed me with a smile.

I raised my hand towards the bag. I smiled. I asked her, "Neha give me water."

But air had blocked her ears. She couldn't hear me. She rolled her eyes and questioned me, "What? I cannot understand you!"

I pulled the bag from her left hand. I removed my T-shirt. I removed a packet from the bag and kept it in it. I picked the water-bottle. I opened the cap and I satisfied my thirst. She picked the deo from my bag. She got up and sprayed it on me. I smelled the deo on my body. It overcame the foul odour. She ran far away from me and I ran behind her. I caught her in my arms. I showered water on her head and on me as well.

Those were memorable romantic days!

NINETEEN

And then to see her, I started attending lectures. Professors were shocked to see me in the class. They asked me, “Do you belong to this class?”

I replied, “Yes Sir!

One professor said, “I am seeing you for the first time in past Seven months!” Everyone in the class laughed.

“So what brings you to attend lectures?

“I want go to grow up!

“You have already grown up! How much more you want to grow?”

"No Sir! I want to grow in studies!"

The whole class laughed.

We both shared the same bench. We always kept a notebook on the bench. If the professor was teaching something, and I had to tell her something; then I used to write on the left page and she used to reply me back on the right page. We shared a wonderful time. I still have that book!

Once we were caught up with each other. The Professor shouted at me.

At my home, I lived in my own world. I used to dream about her all time. We used to chat by messaging each other the whole night. I used to sleep at 2 in the night.

Time flew and I was way behind in my studies! A week later we had our exams. I was occupied by pillars of books.

Soon exams were over. I was stressed so much that I required a break!

My friends organized a picnic and I joined them. They had already warned 'No females!'

Unwillingly I had to leave her alone and go with them. I wanted to meet her but our schedules got overlapped, and we didn't had time for each other. This started disturbing Neha. I was unaware about it! She lost her smile. She ignored me.

Three weeks later our results were hanged on the notice board. Everyone rushed towards it. I had scored pretty well. It was above my expectations. I looked around for Neha. She had seen me from far. She didn't want to come in front of me. She had sent her friend to check her rank. I realized that something was surely wrong. I looked around for her. Her friend said she was on the assembly ground. I pushed across the crowd to meet her.

Many students had gathered there. I tried to peep and see what was going on. I saw Suraj standing in the middle. I saw Neha also standing next to him. She kept her head down and eyes expressionless.

He was speaking something bullshit about our relationship. I looked at Neha. She stood quiet with tears in her eyes. She wiped it. I couldn't bear to see those diamonds falling from her eyes. Everyone around was laughing on her. It was an unbearable situation. I came in front.

He became quiet.

I said, "Neha is not my girl-friend. She is my life! How dare you say anything about her!"

And I slapped him.

Neha looked up. She ran towards me and hanged upon me with her arms around my neck. She wept on my shoulder. The situation was not good but it enriched our relationship.

TWENTY

One day when Neha's brother Shri was going somewhere on his bike, he noticed us on the road. We were walking hand-in-hand. He stopped. He looked at Neha. She was blushing and chatting with me. The same evening when Neha reached home, and she was bombard with questions. She disclosed the truth to Shri. He was annoyed that she had kept mum all these days.

He asked Neha to bring me home. He wanted to meet me. Neha was happy.

She messaged me about this. She said to come home the next day.

The next day, I went to her house. She lived in a row house touching the highway. Like every brother, he tried to explore everything about me! We'll had breakfast together. Neha and I, both, were happy to find his support towards our relationship. We thought it would be very difficult to convince him!

Shri came out to leave me. Suddenly Shri's friends came and circled me. I was unable to understand what was happening. They were holding hockey sticks and stumps and punches. Neha was also confused about what was going on! She was standing at the door. She asked her brother about it. He asked Neha to keep quiet.

So you love my sister!" he approached me, pointing a finger at me. He said aggressively, "Do you think I am a fool!"

I was still not clear what was he talking about!

"What?"

"Ok! You love her, first protect yourself!"

They started beating me. I defended myself against them for a while. But one of them pulled my leg and dropped me down. They stamped me. I started bleeding. Neha came out. She requested her brother to stop. She tried to pull one of them back. But her brother held her back!

I caught a person's leg. And I pulled him down. The people, who were beating me, beat him as well! I used him like a shield and held him firm! And as he got up; I too stood up. I decided, it's enough now! No defense, let's answer them!

And I fought! I even got the custody of Shri, but I left him! Blood ran down my head and my cheek. My arms were bleeding. My shirt was torn.

Shri then admitted me to a nearby hospital. After some days, I got discharged. I went to Shri, I didn't say anything to him. I held Neha's hand and said 'I want to marry Neha."

Shri smiled with tears in his eyes. He said, "I was just testing you. I agree to this marriage." He hugged me.

She became close friends with my parents. Shri and I became good friends. Everyone liked us as a couple.

I then decided I need to work. I need to support my father. Rahul was my good childhood friend. He advised me about Hands on Vision. I joined it! That's a United States collection agency.

For the first time, I met Krishna on the day of the interview. We gave our first round together. The second round was taken on individual basis.

My last round was conducted by Mr. Abhay Chaubey. He was the manager of the process. He was a thin 30-35 year old man with spectacles over his sharp eagle eyes. He moved out of the interview cabin and called my name. I raised my hand. He asked me follow him and I gave an affirmative smile. He went in the cabin. Krishna was nervous and waiting for his round. But greeted me "Best of luck!" And I thanked him in return. I wished him the same as well!

I knocked at the door. And he asked me to come in and grab a seat! He looked at my resume.

I started, "Before you begin sir, may please know your name to address you?"

He looked at me.

"Sure! My name is Abhay Chaubey. I am a part of Operations. So Ajinkya Jadhav, now tell me something about yourself!"

I continued, "I am Ajinkya Jadhav 20 year old residing at Balaji Nagar. I am pursuing last year B. Com." I went on, and on, until he asked me to stop! He was amazed with my confidence. We soon became friends.

He questioned, "Where do you see yourself in 3 years down the line?"

I asked, "What is the eligible criterion of IJP?"

He replied, "18 months!"

I replied to it, "So why will I wait for 3 years! The day I will be eligible for IJP, I will attempt for a senior designation. So, soon I will be at your post!

He admired me, and my confidence; and he appreciated me about it!

Krishna and I cleared the interview together. We became good friends!

I messaged Neha about the good news. My parents celebrated this by gifting me a bike. I had two days to join. I and Neha planned out to go to Panhala; It's a beautiful place near Panvel. We spent a quality time in the midst of the greenery there!

We were 29 people in the training and enjoyed our training. I scored well in all the tests. My intention was to top the score board and I did so!

For a week we were budding with the senior agents. We heard live calls! That's when we learnt ways to tackle various situations! And soon, we were in production.

Mr. Chaubey was trying my patience. For five days he didn't provide him a cubicle to work. But that did not demotivate me.

Soon he gave me a cubicle to login. For the first three days I hatched eggs. I seemed to be a bomb which cannot burst! It's just a dud!

But after those three days, I closed my day on minimum four payments. I was amazingly fast, people complimented.

Two months later, my parents and Neha went for an outing. My leave was put down and so I couldn't join them. They were happy when they left. I never knew that I am watching them smiling for thc last time! Otherwise would have stopped them!

My father drove the car. Neha and my ma sat on the back seat. They crossed the bridge and took the route to the highway. My father drove the car usually at 35 to 40 kilometers per hour. That's an average speed on the highway. The road was empty. A truck was coming at high speed behind them. It was almost 350 meters away. Suddenly it came and collided with the car.

It pushed the car ahead. My father banged his head on the steering wheel. The truck dragged them to a distance of 50 metres. Some people noticed them. They immediately followed the truck and called the cops. The car was smashed completely. My father died on the spot. My mother suffered severe injuries. Neha got head injuries.

They were immediately moved to the nearest hospital. The people found Neha's cell phone in working condition. She had messaged her brother. They gave him a buzz and asked him to come immediately to the hospital. After reaching there, Shri called me up.

Neha was serious and was successfully operated. Neha's family broke. And I lost my parents. I didn't cry to keep my hopes alive!

Today, Neha is in coma. I go to meet her every alternate day in the hospital. Somewhere I have hopes that she'll recover and everything will be fine.

Earlier I was a very jovial person. I used to greet everyone with a smiling face. I had a very good dressing sense. But today I am so stressed that I don't care what I wear and how I look! I have no one for whom I should dress properly!

I feel somewhere down the line, everyone has a purpose of living. I lost my father; I lost my mother. Neha is my love; but today she is in coma. Everyone said she will not come back. I know I will lose her soon, that's the reason maybe I met Kiran? But!

May be I? I am special! So he has chosen me, me to take care of Kiran!

When you don't find the purpose of your life, you should live for others! You should find your dreams in other's dreams! And that's what I will do! I will live for others!

But still there is always a hope as well! I have hopes on him! He, who is sitting high above the clouds, He is watching us. He is trying my patience. I know, He will listen to my prayers!

Kiran and Omkar's eyes were moist. Omkar shut the book.

TWENTY-ONE

Ajinkya was dressing. He was going to work before time. Kiran and Omkar were sitting in the hall watching a movie. Ajinkya came and sat next to Omkar on the couch.

Omkar asked, "So you're ready to go to work."

"Yes!"

"So early?"

"Ya! Listen na?"

Omkar pressed the mute button of the remote. He looked at him.

"Today I am going to apply for IJP!"

"Wow that's great!" said Omkar with joy.

Kiran looked at Omkar. Omkar asked, "But what's that?"

"You're an idiot! Internal Job Posting."

Omkar cut him off, "I said what does that meant? Not the full form!"

"Let me speak! Well, it's like a promotion! You have to give an application to your reporting person and he forwards it to the management. Then, on a particular date, all the candidates have to appear a written test. After some days, second round."

Omkar commented, "Yuck exam! I hate it!"

Ajinkya continued, "Second round is a normal interview round. Three senior management people conduct the third round. They ask process related question and give you some problems. They expect practical and accurate answers. Few days later, the result is out and only one is selected out of the three finalists."

Ajinkya had a thirst for this opportunity. His eyes sparkled and revealed it. He said with confidence, "I am going to apply for the post of Team Leader!"

"Sound's great! Good!"

Ajinkya said, "Neha will be happy to hear that!" A drop fell from his left eye. "Ya!" said Omkar with a soft voice.

Ajinkya prayed with folded hands, "God let my love recover fast please!"

Omkar interrupted him, "Hey, you're getting late! Run!"

He wiped his eyes and said, "Oh ya!" He got up and left the house.

TWENTY-TWO

Bang Birthday Bang

Days passed. Ajinkya had cleared the first round. On Friday he had his second round. That day, he came from the hospital in the afternoon. As soon as he came, he hit the bed. He was tired. He had back-ache. Each bone was paining. But he had to be fresh for the second round which would be conducted by two o'clock in the night.

It was five. Ajinkya was still sleeping. He had to go to work at nine. Kiran was studying in the hall. There was something going on downstairs. Kiran could hear Omkar speaking with someone. He went upstairs with his gang. He knocked at the door. Kiran kept his books on the centre-table. He opened the door. Omkar was standing at the door. He came in and asked for Ajinkya. Kiran said, "He is sleeping."

Omkar replied, "This is not the time to sleep!"

Everyone sat on the couch adjusting for each other. Omkar went in. He thought of something and came back in the hall. He said, "Get ready! Today is my birthday! You have to come!"

He went in the bedroom. Kiran went back and got seated on the couch. He continued his studies. Yash looked into his books.

The bedroom was dark. The curtains were drawn shut. The lights were switched off. Ajinkya was sleeping on the bed with a blanket on him. Omkar pulled Ajinkya from sleep. He tickled and pinched him. But it was of no use. He was not ready to open his eyes. He went in the washroom. He filled a mug with water in it. He went in the hall. He saw Kiran studying.

He ordered Kiran, "Get ready fast! Go now!" Kiran closed the book. He went in the bedroom. He picked his clothes and went in the washroom to change. Yash said, "But Omkar! Your birthday is two months later right?"

Omkar replied, "I know my birthday very well!" He went in the bedroom. He splashed water on Ajinkya.

He woke up. He asked frustrated, "Uff! What happened yaar?" "It's my birthday! How can you sleep! C'mon I have to cut the cake!"

He pulled Ajinkya's hand and took him to the hall. He pulled him from his house. They were accompanied by Kiran and Omkar's friends.

Ajinkya said, "Wait man! Look at me. How can I come in a night suit yaar. Let me go up and dress up!" "No! Let it be."

"Wait let me buy a gift for you!"

"No! Not required."

They reached Omkar's home. He made Ajinkya sit on the chair. Kiran sat next to him. Everyone got seated on the couch. Omkar latched the door. He went in the kitchen. The hall was decorated with red blue and yellow ribbons. At the four corners balloons were stuck. A big balloon was stuck right below the fan. Everyone was there, expect Rahul. Ajinkya doubted something was wrong. How could he forget his best friend's birthday? Maybe these days he was forgetting many things!

Omkar's mother came out. She greeted everyone. She was wearing a red saree He went in. Omkar pulled the centre-table. She brought the cake out. The cake was still packed. Omkar placed the cake on the centre-table.

Everyone circled the table. Everyone was eager to see the design of the cake. Some of them peeped from the edge of the box. They could only see pink colour. Omkar pulled Ajinkya and Kiran in front. He went near the cake. His mother gave him knife and candle. He kept it on the table.

Omkar went near and said to Kiran, "I have seen your birth certificate." He smiled. Ajinkya was amazed. Kiran became nervous. Omkar said, "Kiran, Happy Birthday! Will you become our friend?"

Omkar's mother unpacked the cake. The cake had a brown house on a pink lotus which greeted "Happy Birthday Kiran"

This is the drawing which Omkar discovered from Kiran's bag while investigation.

Tears brimmed in Kiran's eyes. He hugged Omkar. Kiran wept on his shoulder. He smiled. Everyone clapped for Omkar. He gave his best to become Kiran's friend. This was great thing for a kid who was all alone in this world! That's love! Ajinkya said, "It's beautiful!"

Omkar whispered in Kiran's ears, "I love you! Don't worry I will not tell anyone what I know about you!"

He gave the knife in Kiran's hand. Omkar explained to her what to do.

Kiran blew the candle. Ajinkya burst the balloon right above Kiran's head. Everyone sang, "Happy Birthday to you!"

Kiran drove the knife into the cake. He gave the first bite to Ajinkya. Ajinkya gave a piece in his mouth; he then gave a bite to Omkar and then to his mother. Omkar took a piece and applied on Kiran's face.

Kiran cried, stop it!

His mother took the cake and went in the kitchen. Ajinkya went in the kitchen to help Aunty. Some sat on the couch; some on the carpet. Kiran went to the wash his face. Omkar played a music cd. Kiran came in the hall.

Ajinkya served a plate of eatables to everyone. There was a piece of cake, some wafers, chuda and two chocolates. After serving everyone, Ajinkya and Aunty took a plate for themselves. Everyone was enjoying the time together. Aunty inquired, "So Ajinkya I heard you cleared the first round of IJP!"

"Yes I did!"

"When is the next round?"

"Today!"

"So are you prepared?"

"Yes I am! And today is the second round!"

"That's great!"

"Best of luck!"

"Thanks!" He smiled.

"Omkar wanted to give a surprise to everyone. He told me about it. We planned this evening. See, he decorated the house. He didn't allow me to help him!"

Ajinkya said, "he seems to have grownup now! You have made a very good cake!"

She smiled and replied, "Thanks!"

Ajinkya said, "He is totally mad. See he picked me from the bed!"

She smiled.

Ajinkya looked at the watch. He said, "Aunty I need to leave. Bye!"

"Ok! And best of luck!"

"Thanks Aunty!"

TWENTY-THREE

A week passed and the day came for the final round. Ajinkya got up early. He got ready. He went to the temple, came back, prepared breakfast and also lunch for Kiran. Omkar came. Ajinkya was wearing shoes. He asked, "Bhaiya, I came and you're going!"

"No man! I am going to the hospital. Today is the final round."

"So you will go to office directly from there?"

"Yes! I have prepared the lunch for you and Kiran. Just tell aunty to take care of Kiran's dinner. OK?"

"Sure!"

Ajinkya left. Kiran and Omkar had breakfast. They played computer games. They enjoyed the time they spent to together. He taught Kiran how to use computer!

Omkar said, "So Kiran! Have you planned to open up?"

"I cannot dare to do that!"

"Remember then you're cheating everyone! And that will not benefit anyone! You still have time!" He kept quiet. He continued, "I don't know the complete story! But I know something about it! I have faith in you. Go ahead!"

Rahul came home. He saw Omkar and Kiran playing video game in the hall. He removed his shoes and socks. He kept it behind the door in the shoe-rack. He asked for tea. His mother gave him a cup of hot tea. He sat on the couch. He watched them playing.

Suddenly, Rahul's phone buzzed. He answered the phone. He replied shockingly, "What? I am coming Ajinkya!"

Rahul disconnected the phone. He kept the cup on the center table. He went to the door. He kept the cell phone on the dining table. He quickly wore socks and shoes. He took his cell phone.

Omkar asked "What's wrong bhaiya?"

Rahul replied, "Bad news! Neha departed this world an hour ago. I need to rush to her place!"

Omkar and Kiran were stunned. Omkar said, "Take me bhaiya!"

Rahul tried to dissuade him but failed. Rahul, Omkar and Kiran left for Neha's place.

An ambulance arrived in the society carrying Neha's body on a stretcher. Ajinkya and Shri came along. The ward-boys placed the stretcher in the parking. Krishna came ahead of the crowd. Neha's Father, Krishna, Ajinkya and Shri took it over their shoulders. They took it to their home. Neha's family was drowned in sorrow. Her body was moved to the Crematorium. The men followed. Kiran was shocked and had no courage to follow them.

The burning wood was transferred to Shri. Shri took it and went to Ajinkya. He said, "Ajinkya this is your right!"

He glanced at Shri. A drop fell from Ajinkya's tear-filled eyes. He lit the pyre. He hugged Shri wept. He hugged Neha's father. Neha's mother was crying since she heard this news. The society women were sitting around her and trying to console her.

Shri said to Ajinkya, "I know you loved her a lot! But remember she wanted to see you rising up. Today is the final round. You have to win it! You have worked hard! You have to get ready!"

He convinced Ajinkya and they came back home.

Ajinkya took a shower. He sat below the shower naked. He committed, I will not cry till I achieve my goal: the post of Team Leader!

He punched the wall to some of his anger. But he cried with pain, I will not cry! I will place my anger aside and would use my best skills and achieve it!

But still he had overcome with tears, his hopes shattered like a piece of glass.

He reached the office. People in his office knew about his situation. He logged in. Everyone was tense for him.

He calmed himself. He got control on his thoughts! He drank water to clear his throat. He closed his eyes to firm himself. The first call came his way.

The worst call!

The costumer was pissed off and his anger was on the top of the sky.

Manager and Sachin Patil came to know that The Client from United States had jumped into random live call monitoring. And the worst part was they were listening to the conversation between Ajinkya and the customer!

It's called live call barging, which rarely happened! Clients don't carry emotions or relations at work! If they find something wrong, then they flag it and termination comes into picture!

Ajinkya being unaware about it, he knew to take control on the call and calm the costumer, he needs to calm down first! His eyes were still closed! He opened his eyes. A stream of tears ran down from his red eyes, like the River Ganga flows down the Great Himalayas.

Mr. Chaubey, Sachin Patil and the Quality team head quickly jumped into the call and barged the screen as well!

The next thing to worry came in place! The quality head opened up quality sheet to gagged him.

Customer blabbered for almost twelve minutes. In this only Ajinkya attempted to interrupt him. Quality marked down for interruption! Lost five points!

Customer finally stopped and there Ajinkya left a dead air. Customer after few seconds inquired, Are you there?

Quality marked him down there as well! Lost another five points! You may lose customer from the call and that's why it's a mark down!

Ajinkya replied, Yes I am there! I was left speechless when I was listening your experience! I am sorry to hear about your loss of husband!

Quality erased the markdown of dead air as Ajinkya smartly played with his words!

Ajinkya continued, Sorry to hear that you tried to help your grand-daughter, and you gave a connection under your name! Sorry to hear that she refuses to pay it as she is in college and now this bill is bothering you and your credit!

He paused! He looked at the screen. The customer's account had popped up! But his eyes were burning and he was unable to look at the screen! Mr. Nayak stood up and looked out from his glass cabin to see what he was doing! Ajinkya was sitting just like forty steps away from his cabin. He murmured speak up Ajinkya! Speak up my friend!

Ajinkya rubbed his eyes as hard could! He rubbed his palms together and then transferred the warmth to his eyes!

Now it was his time blabbered as he knew he was taking time and to avoid customer taking over the call he needs to speak!

I apologize mam, today you're all alone and the only source of income you have is social security! I love my mom a lot! My mom passed away few months back! I don't remember when, maybe because she is still alive in my heart! She is my inspiration! If I would have been your grandson, I wouldn't have left you alone! I miss my grand-mom I never saw her except in photos!

The lady reacted, Oh!

He took a deep breath and he continued, but the fact is the bill exists under your name! As you mentioned the cell-phone company refuses to cooperate! I will not ask you to pay the bill in one go! I can offer you a payment plan!

They built a mutual understanding and Ajinkya earned 95 in quality. The client marked an appreciation mail to the Mr. Nayak immediately! The stress face of the Mr. Nayak gained a smile!

He walked to Sachin's desk. Sachin got up from his seat, Sir!

He whispered to Sachin, All credit goes to Ajinkya! Forget IJP, many such will come and go but today if he had done any silly mistakes then would have lost his job!"

He used his smart brain and contributed his part to the portfolio; unexpected wonder happened!

TWENTY-FOUR

It was two o'clock by his wrist watch. The final round had begun. One by one, each candidate went in the conference room. A session went for almost 35 minutes. He was the last candidate to go for the round. He was asked to log in.

Soon his turn came. His Team Leader, Sachin Patil commanded, "Ajinkya, log out!" He logged out. He went to Sachin's desk. Sachin said to him, "Get ready! It's now your turn!" Sachin and Ajinkya both were nervous about the round.

Ajinkya went to the washroom. He emptied his bladder. With the fluid, his stress and tension disappeared too. He stood in front of the mirror. He looked at his reflection. His body language still displayed his stress. Rahul came in. He went near the urinal cubicle. He looked at Ajinkya's reflection on the wall-tiles.

Rahul said, "Ajinkya wash your face and comb your hair properly!" Ajinkya walked to the wash basin. He splashed water on his face. He rubbed his face. He stood straight. He again looked at his reflection. Rahul walked to the wash basin. He washed his hands. Ajinkya pulled out a couple of tissues and wiped his face. His stress got stuck on the tissue like the dirt on his face. He felt better, but still his head felt heavy like a stone. Rahul combed his hair. He adjusted Ajinkya's shirt and pants. Dust had formed a layer over his shoes. He wiped his sharp pointed black formal shoes. He walked out of the washroom.

He went to his Team Leader. He spoke less but he sounded confident. Sachin said, "Sit down!" He gave Ajinkya some tips. An office boy came searching him. He is called for the round. He walked to the conference room. He halted near the glass non-transparent door. He looked at his reflection and gave a smile and then he knocked at the door.

A voice said, "Come in!"

Ajinkya went in. He saw Mr. Chaubey sitting there. He was accompanied by Mr. Pare, Pune Division-Head of House of Vision and an unknown senior management person named, Mr. Nayak. He greeted them. He drew a smile on emotionless and stressed face. Mr. Chaubey glanced at his face. His face revealed his stress and pain. Mr. Pare said "Have a seat!" Mr. Chaubey asked, "Are you sure, Mr.

Jadhav that you will be able to go through this questionnaire round? Because I came to know the situation you went through today afternoon!"

He swallowed his sour spit down and said, "I am fine! Let the rounds be tougher. I want check my caliber!"

Sachin bit his nails between his teeth with tension. Almost 40 minutes later, Ajinkya came out. He was quiet and calm. He went back to his system and got logged-in. After an hour of discussion, the management people went back to their respective work.

Ajinkya came back to home. There was darkness in the whole house. He could see someone sleeping on the couch. From the height he recognised Kiran. He sat on the couch, removed his shoes and recollected everything what happened since morning! He lost himself in the darkness around.

TWENTY-FIVE

Two weeks later, after the first shift logged out everyone gathered in the front office room. A couple of agents were logged in. Today, the results were to be out! All the three candidates had their expectations on high. Mr. Chaubey came out and there remained a pin-drop silence. He said, "Today we have gathered here to announce update about our market ranking. I heartily thank everyone present here for giving your best; you have pushed our competitors down for third consecutive time in rankings! We are Number One, for the third in row!" There was a big applause, after which Mr. Pare came ahead and took over the session. He said "Guys thank you for your contribution to this company! We heartily thank you! Well we have the announcement of RnR!"

RnR means Rewards and Regrets. This is a felicitation programme where the Highest Collectors are greeted and highlighted in the company.

Mr. Pare announced, "Ajinkya is rewarded with Best Collector for consecutive two months!" The RnR session went on for almost next ten minutes. Everyone was excited to know who had cleared the IJP. All the three candidates were strong. Mr. Chaubey came ahead.

He had an envelope in his hand. He looked at it. Later, he said, "It was a tough session of IJP. The three finalists please come up!"

The three finalists came out from the crowd and stood next to Mr. Chaubey. Their heart started pumping fast. Ajinkya stood between the two. He continued, "Everyone here is talented, that's why you are called Bill Collector! Right?"

The crowd replied, "Yes!"

He said, "When it came to choose one out of these, it was very difficult! In terms of points, they had a difference of what, 34 points to 40 points between their rankings. But we were looking for a person whose one mistake will eliminate him; and exactly the same happened. After that, we only saw their thinking and we shortlisted one out of the two. Let's see the result!"

He opened the envelope. He removed a white piece of paper from it. He unfolded it. The candidates were nervous. The excitement level rose to its pitch! He saw the name. He said in a loud voice, "Out of these three guys, there is a guy who had challenged me when I took his interview that he will achieve a senior post soon! Due to some reason he was late to appear for the IJP. But in his first IJP he was shortlisted for the final round!" Ajinkya looked down. He continued "And he has proved it!"

Mr. Nayak kept quiet. No one reacted. The two finalists realized that they have lost it. Images of the last interview and Cremation flashed into front of Ajinkya's eyes. The two standing next to him tapped his shoulder. Ajinkya recalled himself to reality. He looked up. His eyes were red. He was feeling sleepy. He has not slept for the past four days. He was just waiting for the result. He went to Mr. Chaubey. Tears ran down his cheeks. He shook hand with Mr. Nayak hugged him. He wept. Mr. Chaubey tapped his back. Ajinkya wiped his eyes. He turned to the crowd. The crowd cheered loudly. He shook hand with Mr. Pare. Mr. Pare said, "Congratulation! You have bagged the post. You are now Team Leader of the same Portfolio for which he used to take calls!" The session ended. Mr. Chaubey said, "Shift One is asked to move out! Shift Two log in guys, back to collections guys!"

Ajinkya was assigned a team of ten collectors. Krishna and Rahul both were in his team. He was asked to report in Shift One and had to report to Mr. Chaubey.

TWENTY-SIX

Ajinkya went through very tough times of his life! He was tired and very stressed. So he requested for two days leave which was accepted!

He decided to go and meet his old friends. He contacted a few of them. By afternoon, he became free.

It was the last working day of the month. Many schools had a half day. Ajinkya went to Omkar's school. He drove his 2-wheeler. Omkar was happy to see Ajinkya in his school. Almost eight months later he had come to Omkar's school to pick him up.

Months later Omkar had seen Ajinkya smiling. Omkar sat on his bike and they left.

Ajinkya took him to a nearby restaurant. It was a good restaurant. There were small brown huts with conical roofs of red tiles; and each hut was surrounded by a garden. Each hut had a marble round table with three brown light-weight wooden chairs. They walked in. They checked at the entrance. They skipped a couple of huts and went in the Fourth hut from the entrance. Omkar asked his favourite cuisine 'Chinese'. They had it; and then they had ice-cream. And Omkar's stomach was full.

By 4, they were back. Ajinkya dropped him in the parking of his society. Omkar walked towards the stairs. Ajinkya sat on his bike. Omkar came back to Ajinkya.

Omkar asked, "Where is Kiran?"

Ajinkya replied, "He has gone for his tuitions!" He looked at his wrist watch and said, "He will be back in thirty minutes."

Omkar kept quiet for a minute. He said, "Bhaiya I suppose he is still hiding something from us!"

A question popped in Ajinkya's mind. He tried to search the answer by running a search in his past memories. He then inquired, "Why do you think so?"

Omkar was numb again. He sat besides Ajinkya.

He said, "Bhaiya, he sometime behaves very different. He stays between us, but still he is mentally not present sometimes. Something is wrong! (He took a minute pause) There is a strong power in his eyes. I like him!"

Ajinkya replied, "Don't worry, I will look into it. And don't worry, I will fix it Omkar!"

Omkar turned back and climbed couple of stairs. He looked back and said to him with a smile, "ok, I am getting late! Need to go ! Bye."

Ajinkya replied, "Bye!"

TWENTY-SEVEN

Ajinkya went back home. He went to the washroom to wash his face. He sat on the couch and started reading the newspaper.

About ten minutes later, he heard a knock at his door. He opened the door. Kiran was standing at the door. He came in and went in the bedroom. He kept his bag at its place. He washed his hands and feet. Ajinkya relaxed on the couch. Kiran washed his face and changed his clothes. He came and sat on the couch. He looked at Ajinkya. He was busy trailing the news.

Kiran uttered in a numb voice, "Bhaiya, I have something to share with you!"

Ajinkya looked at him. He folded the newspaper and kept it on the centre table. Ajinkya looked at him with a happy smiley face.

Kiran started, "You always say start a relation should be on the basis of truth?! I am a liar. I lied to you. And now I want to acknowledge it! Today I want to unwind my past and present!" Kiran spoke with a bold voice but was hesitating to continue. Ajinkya gave a smile.

Kiran continued, "I lived far away from this place with my parents. Our house was as small as a match-box. We lived in one single room with mud walls and a roof made of tin sheet. It was too suffocating! We lived in a rented house. My parents were poor. I don't remember their names. I had two elder sisters and two young sisters. Tina and Smita of age ten and thirteen. Jyoti and Simran were my two younger sisters of five and three. I had long hair. I always tied two plaits.

My father always wanted to have a baby boy; a child who would carry the family name ahead. He always tried to avoid us. He worked in a four wheeler factory. He used to get paid every 7th of the month. And by the time 25th came, he had no money. He gave my mother some money to run the house which was barely sufficient. So she started making garlands of plastic flowers. For twenty garlands she got thirty rupees. It took almost twenty minutes for my mother to make one. She was an inspiration for me to believe that one day my life would change for the better. We also helped and we stored the money saved in a plastic compass box. My father didn't know about that.

He never brought new clothes and food for us. He sometimes used to booze and come home. He used to beat my mother with his belt.. He used to beat us as well. We used to wear torn clothes.

I can only remember his brutal face! I hated my life, but I knew one day our life would change! I had big dreams, but I knew it couldn't be converted into reality. I wanted to study. I wanted to become a famous identity. My mother wanted to go to school when she was small but her mother did not let her go. So she always wanted us to be educated.

My elder sisters, Tina and Smita went to afternoon school. I, Jyoti and Simran went to the school in the morning, Monday to Friday and in the afternoon on Saturday. Our school was at a distance of thirty minutes from our house. We traveled bare foot on the kachcha road to reach our two floors school building and it had only one ground in front. There were a couple of trees around it!

We would have that assembly on the ground. We formed two lines standard-wise, one for boys and one for girls. Our teachers conducted the prayers, pledge and national anthem. Everyday three students of one standard had to come up and read the prayer. Then we were sent standard-wise to our respective classrooms.

In our classroom there were no benches. All round there were charts on the wall with different pictures. One had 'A' and had an apple drawn next to it. One chart also had numbers and candles next to it. There was a black-board and one table and chair for the teacher.

The routine timetable was first four lectures then a fifteen minutes break and after that, six lectures with a thirty minute lunch break. Our school used to provide poha during lunch break.

My mother could afford some biscuits for my Lunch Box. I felt shy to have it front of my friends, so I sat alone away from them in a corner. I used to have only two of them. And rest I kept in my frock pocket. I ate them during lectures.

One day during a science period, when we all were sitting down, I took a bite of the biscuit. Our school bag was to our right and lunch bag to the left. Everyone had a book open on the lap and a notebook. The teacher was writing something on the black-board. She heard the sound. She looked back. I looked down. I was the only one looking down. She asked me to look up. I kept the biscuit below my tongue. I looked up. She said, "Why are you not writing?"

I kept quiet. I was unable to speak because of the biscuit. She asked twice, and then she understood that I had something in my mouth. She asked me to come near her. She kept the chalk on the table. She asked me to open the mouth. I opened. She saw the brown liquid in my mouth. She shouted and scolded me in front of the whole class.

I started crying and my sound was audible to the last class in the corridor. Everyone looked at me, some closed their ears. She looked around. Everyone was annoyed with the wailing sound. She went to the table. She opened her purse, removed a chocolate and gave it to me and asked me sit quietly. I wiped my tears. I went back to my place. I opened the wrapper and put the chocolate in my mouth. Around noon, I went back home with my younger sisters. It wasn't really a bad life and I used to enjoy learning.

TWENTY-EIGHT

But one fine day my father said it was no use educating us since we were girls. So he cancelled our names from the school register. My mother kept our documents in a safe place. And father was unaware about it. She had hopes that someday down the line he would realize his mistake.

He used to throw us out of the house and fuck my mother. She used get beaten up frequently. Those scenes created a huge impact on our minds. I could see the same scenes in my dreams as well. I didn't know what was enjoyable in it!

I told my mother many times, let's run away! At the first go, she always agreed. But later, she said with a sad voice, 'He is my husband. For me he is my God; I cannot leave him alone and go! She had dreams to see us become respectable adults!

Time passed. My mother went into depression. She was a wife and a mother. She was compelled to agree with her husband on every point; he couldn't care less about her children's future. She wished to see us grow and live happily. But what we achieved was poverty, stress and depression. She advised us to run away.

We used to decide to run down to the city. My mother packed our bags, but we never could leave our mother and go.

That evening, my father came home early. He was fully drunk. He was unable to walk properly. My mother was busy cooking food for dinner. We were sitting to a side and playing ludo. We were giggling and laughing. A romantic song was played on radio kept next to us.

He came in, locked the door. I looked at him. I tried to avoid him. It was my chance to throw the dice. I threw the dice on him. I heard my mother's cry. I looked back. She was lying at the corner. Blood ran down from her head. We were frightened seeing that.

He warned her, "madarchod. Now, I want a boy. Remember, I want a boy to make me stand proud in the society. Or else, I will sell you to my friend!"

Jyoti and Simran started crying. I tried to control them. My brains were not working. What should I do! Console my small sisters or save my mother?

He caught her in his arms. She was crying in pain. Her eyes were closed. He pulled off her saree from her body. He tore her blouse with his both hands. He tried to open the knot of her petticoat. He couldn't open it. He dropped her down. Her head banged on the floor. She shouted, "Help me! I will die! Help me!"

I could hear noise all round! My sisters were crying; my elder sisters shouting; and my mother crying in pain. I closed both my ears with my hands. The world around me started rotating. I was fed up with this!

He searched for a knife. He found it below the chopped vegetables near the burning chulha. He chopped off the knot. He threw the knife. It fell between the burning chulha. He pulled off her white skirt. He then stripped off his shirt. He threw it to one corner. He pulled the zip of his pant down. He went on his knees. He slept on her. She was still crying in pain. He said 'I am sorry!' He slowly moved his hot palm over her breast. He caught her breast in his palm. He pressed and moved it. She calmed down. He then, sucked milk from her breast. She kept quiet.

But I couldn't see this scene anymore. I took my bag over my shoulder. I asked my sister to help me. But they all were frightened! I went ahead. I looked around. I saw a hammer lying on the floor at one corner. I picked it up. I went near him. I raised my hand to beat him with the hammer. I hated him a lot, but still I loved him, he was my father! How can I hit him? A question quickly popped up.

For a minute, I was confused. Soon, I overcame the flow of emotions in me. I struck the hammer on his back, but maybe like my strength disappeared. I couldn't hit him hard.

He looked at me. He got up. He picked me up. I tried to get out of his hands, but I couldn't. He opened the door. I looked at my mother. She gathered some strength and got up. She opened her eyes with pain. Her eyes were fully red with blood. She looked around. She took the burning wood from the chulha.

He threw me out of the house. And he locked the door. People had gathered at the door. I went to the window to see in. My mother threw the burning wood on him. I asked help from the people standing around. She looked at me and shouted, "Run, Kiran. Run!"

I heard my mother's voice. It banged my ear-drums with lightning speed. The vibrations buzzed an alarm and my brain commanded my legs immediately, "Run!"

Instantly the command was followed without any second thought. My body parts geared up. My heart pumped blood with greater speed.

My legs slowly turned back. They started walking away from my house. Gradually they picked up speed in multiples. I didn't knew where I was going, but still I was running!

I could hear a mixture of voice, my ma saying run Kiran, a motorcycle passing, a man sitting on his charpai and chanting waheguru waheguru; azaan conducted in a mosque nearby; an evening mass being conducted in a church on my way; someone chanting hanuman chalisa, kids playing and women gossiping; someone cutting a wood. And loud radio which played, 'zindagi ka safar hai kesa safar koi...'

I crossed many houses of known and unknown people. But I was not in my senses to ask help from them. I crossed many shops. I ran through the kachcha - pucca roads and streets with my bare feet.

I crossed a couple of street lamps. I pushed the crowd to a side. I heard many people shouting and speaking, a radio jockey was speaking on some radio channel. I was unable to control my legs. I went in front of two-three vehicles. They instantly applied brakes to prevent the accident. They shouted, "Hey, are you mad? Die somewhere else!"

I wiped my running tears. My brain was just commanding, "Run! Run fast!!"

My brain was not ready to listen to my heart. The crowd shouted at me. Ignoring them, I walked for a couple of minutes. Then again I gathered up speed. Emotions were flowing down my cheeks in the form of tears. I wiped them with my palm. I was not happy. I was running away from my house, leaving my mother and my sisters in trouble.

I reached a good distance from my place. I looked back. I could see everything blurred. I wiped my eyes. My house was on fire. I could see people shouting. My mother's voice was still resonating in my mind.

My legs took the route back to my house but I stopped mid-way. I thought about my mother who had high ambitions for my future. Staying there I would not be able to do that. So I hated my life, but I was given a chance to change it! 'Why are you acting foolish?' asked my heart.

I left my village. I reached a nearby town. I was tired and hungry. My hands were sticky. I washed it at a sweet mart. Then I sat under a tree.

I pulled off the bag from my shoulder. I opened it. I found some of my documents. I saw my birth certificate and leaving certificate of my previous school. I found my school picnic photograph and my drawing book. There were some clothes as well. I found a carry bag. I opened it. There were two chapatis and an onion.

Looking at it, I couldn't control my hungry stomach. I grabbed it with my dirty hands. I swallowed it in hurry, and I swallowed like the starving snake swallows the rat.

I was shivering with cold and I was tense, 'Now what? What next?'

'Where will I stay?' I cried.

'What will I eat?' I cried again.

Suddenly, I looked up and a kid caught my sight. He was doing some work in a factory under the bright yellow light hanging above his head. I could see many children working there. I comprehended, 'It looks like a factory, imitation jewelry factory! I didn't knew that kids are hired now it seems that my dreams will come true!'

I crawled with my frozen feet and went in the huge factory. There were many tables and many children working in. I walked on the empty passage between them. The room had florescent orange lights all around. I looked at the person, maybe the manager, sitting on the wooden chair. I walked to him and I said to him with a soft voice, "Excuse me!" He looked at me.

He stood up and asked, "What are you doing here?"

I requested, "Sir I require work! I want to work!" he looked at me. He kept a tooth pick between his lips.

He interviewed, "Where have you come from?" I explained that I need money and shelter. He nodded and said, "I like your spirit! But once anyone comes here he cannot go back from here! Think once again!"

I confidently replied, "No I will work here!"

"Ok!" He said, "You can live here! You will get four times food and twice you will get tea. You can stay here!"

He called, "Ramu!" His voice banged in the whole factory and came back to him.. A white haired scaly person wearing a sleeveless vest and a pant folded up to his knees and with a towel on his right shoulder, came to him running. He joined hands and stood in front of him.

He asked Ramu, "Check his bag!" Ramu pulled the bag from my shoulder. He unzipped and check the bag thoroughly. Ramu said, "Nothing sir!" He said to me, "Ok Show her the room and get her here I will show her the work." I followed Ramu to the room. I walked with pride. Now I could earn and study! 'And now my way is clear', that's what I thought!

Two months passed. I learnt a lot of things there. And almost everyone became my friend there. There was continuous increase in work load! So, I was unable to study. I came to know that this was not a sudden rise. The manager increased the demand so that they remained engaged in work. There was always a race to go ahead of the other.

We prepared copper jewelry there. And we worked in three teams. My stress was increased day-by-day. And I soon got addicted to cigarette! As time passed by, I became impatient day-by-day.

For them, this was their world and did not want to go beyond this factory. Couple of them tried to run away, but none succeeded. Kids who were caught were brutally beaten with red hot road. Later they were kept separate from rest of the kids for couple of days in a small room naked with big fat rats, under a 120 watt bulb. These rats used to eat some of their flesh and make the wound fresh. After some days the wounds were covered by a piece of cloth and they were thrown back between the others. This frightened everyone and no one dared again. But I decided I won't give up.

Shreyash, a 14 year old friend of mine had the same thought of escape from this hell. But the question for us was how to do that?

For a week, we monitored the routine of work. Ramu got up early around 4 P.M. and then he awaked the others. One by one, everyone took a bath and got ready. We prepared the breakfast and finished it by 6 P.M. At 9 P.M. manager arrived and we used to sit back at our places and started our work. At 11 P.M., we had our dinner and then back to work. During these periods, it was difficult to escape. But at 3 A.M., when we went to sleep, somewhere it was possible. After we went to sleep, Ramu used to take a round and then he used to go to sleep. On the main door, there was a lock and it had two keys, one with the manager and the other was always with Ramu. But we decided, at any cost a week later we will escape.

It was a Thursday morning! Wednesday was just over and everyone was tried and went to sleep. Suresh switched off the light. I slept next to Shreyash. A while later there was dark peace all around. He got up slowly. We had fifteen minutes in hand to pack our bags.

Fifteen minutes later, Ramu walked in. we both moved back to our place. I closed my eyes and took the blanket over. He looked around. Everyone was deep asleep. He left.

We got up and loaded our bags on our shoulder and walked to the door. We went in Ramu's room. It was a small room. There were couple of empty beer bottles kept lining to the wall. Shreyash walked towards him and stood next to the door. He took the main door key. He walked a grasshopper walking on the water.

He opened the door. We slowly pushed the door back. Shreyash pushed me ahead. I doubted that something would go wrong. So I turned back! Shreyash pushed me front and asked me to look ahead!

In between of this drama the handle of my bag stuck in the latch and the door banged. I ran out and Shreyash ran in. he dropped the key near the door. Ramu got up. Shreyash moved back in the room where everyone was sleeping. Ramu walked to the door. I removed my bag quickly and disappeared. He opened the door and peeped out. He did not find anyone. He locked the door and went in to check it everything was fine.

I ran from there as fast as could. I felled many times on my way; I got up and again started running. Soon I reached a S.T. stand and saw a dabba. There were few sardars having cup of tea there. I missed the bus. It departed for Swargate. I walked to the dabba. I sprinkled water on my face. The Sardar said to his friend, "Oye Jasbeer chal oye! Der ho rahi he! By morning we need to reach Swargate."

I walked to them. I said, "Excuse me Sardarji!"

He glanced at me and my dirty frock. He said, "Yes!"

I said, "I have missed the bus! My mother is boarding that bus! Can you take me to Swargate?"

He monitored me from top to bottom. I said, "I need your help please sardarji! Help me! I need to go back to my mother!"

He questioned, "But where do you want to go?"

I replied, "Swargate!"

"Where in Swargate?" he questioned again.

"My aunt lives in the apartment in front of P.M.T bus stop!" I comprehended again.

I begged to the Sardarji to take me away from here. Usually, Sardars are soft-hearted, and so was he! He brought me to Swargate in his trust. I don't know what he saw in me that without asking me anything, he gave me lift in his lorry.

He consoled me, "Ok fine, I will take you!"

Jasbeer, the Sardar and I sat in the lorry and left. I was tried and went to sleep on jasbeer's shoulder.

He dropped me at the main bus stop of Swargate. I was tired and could not keep my eyes open any longer. And fell down and went deep asleep.

TWENTY-NINE

The new dawn

Few hours later, 25 year old guy dressed formally walked by. He picked me up and offered me a glass of water. He wiped my face. But still I couldn't breakthrough my sleep. He kept a twenty rupee note in my hand and left. He resembled like the God's messenger and spread light all around! He walked down the street and gradually disappeared!

Few days I lived on the street. Then I decided one day to visit some schools and inquire about the admission.

I went to a couple of schools dressed in new clothes. I spoke with the Headmasters there. I expressed my greed of completing education. They saw my documents. They asked, "Ok! Come with your parents. We will speak about it!" Then, I told them about my past. And they straightaway refused to give me admission!

I went to a couple of schools. I spoke with the Headmasters there. I expressed my greed of completing education. They saw my documents. They asked, "Ok! Come with your parents. We will speak about it!" Then, I told them about my past. And they straightaway refused to give me admission!

I was frustrated. I was tired. This was a big slap to my ego. I said to myself, 'maybe I don't have education in my luck; and my life is really a curse! I sat on the ground. I looked around and I saw children playing. Boys were enjoying their football, while girls were playing basketball. Then, suddenly I could hear children in the classroom reciting tables. My desire to study overwhelmed me. Unknowingly I also started reciting it! That's where I learnt tables of fifteen. I said to myself 'its fine! I will work and will come to the school ground. I will listen to the children studying. I will learn in this same manner which will not charge me fees. After all, a degree is just for name; my work will be my certificate! And I will have practical life knowledge!'

Every day I used to go there and stand on the ground and listen to children studying. But later, my entrance was prohibited. I started falling short of money. I decided to resume work. I wandered the whole day for work, but everything went in vain. I sat on a bench in a garden. On the other side the sun set. A cold breeze was blowing in the garden. People were relaxed. Children were playing see-saw.

The frustration in me started killing me. I looked at the green carpet below my feet. I saw the blooming flowers which surrounded me all over. They attracted me and pulled away the negativity. I soon calmed down.

A twelve year old boy was sitting next to me. He looked at me. He spoke to me. Soon we became friends. I narrated the whole story to him. His name was Javed.

He said, "I can give you work, but?"

I asked with a soft voice, "but what?"

He said, "The shop-owner will not keep a girl at work. You have to change your attire a bit. You have to become a boy."

He took me to a barber. The barber chopped my hair. We went to buy some clothes. I bought it with my money. A couple of pants and two half- shirts! He taught me how to remove a male voice. He took me to Salim. Salim Khan was the owner of a tea stall. He worked in an IT company and tea stall business was a side-business for him. Javed spoke with Salim about me. He said I required work. Salim agreed to give me work. Javed promised to teach me the work; since I didn't know anything.

Javed said to me, "Forget whatever happened in past its gone. Work first, earn money and then you will get what you wish! This world runs on money!" I nodded my head in affirmation to him.

I was happy. I had a reason to live! I lived happily with Javed. I shared my joy and sorrow with him. Salim lived in a flat at a distance. We lived in a tent next to the tea-stall. An open space near the canal was our toilet. There was a government common washroom nearby. I used to go there. Since I lived a life of a boy, I could not step in the girl's washroom. Usually, we bathed together. He enjoyed watching me. He locked me in his arms every day. He enjoyed me. That was when I understood what happens when someone loves you; you tend to forget your stress, your problems! You live with a different joy. I allowed him to kiss me as he had helped me a lot; but didn't allow him to sleep with me.

I dididn't like the work, but I dididn't want a change of my place of work, since I was tired of running from one place to another and I enjoyed Javed's company. By evening, I used to get tired, so Javed taught me how to inhale whitener. It used to destress me. Sometimes we used to steal cigarette or gutka. We use to enjoy having that as well! I trusted Javed always. I gave everything to this tea stall.

But soon, I realized how foolish I was! Salim treated me as a servant. He always looked for his benefit. Javed just enjoyed me like a call girl that too for free! They were nowhere different than the factory manager!

And then, I met you. First I feared to trust you. But as time passed, I started trusting you. And now I have unveiled my entire past to you today!

I know Child Labour is a crime! But, no one wants to know the reason for it. Children love to enjoy their life and love to play! Then why is a child working?

The answer is, because adults, especially parents, are not doing their job properly! Even in cities, I see parents with daughters and sons sending the sons to an English Medium school while the girls study in Marathi Medium. This is where we err! If these are educated people, then we uneducated people are better than them!

I see beggars whose hands and legs are fine, but they still beg! They are lazy and careless about their children's future.

This world is selfish! It does not care for others! I had lost hopes of something good to happen! I was always just consoling myself. I didn't expect this miracle to happen and someone like you, to come into my life, and help me!

I am Kiran Kulkarni and I am proud to be a girl. The condition at that time forced me to become a boy! We are accidentally twins! He was a boy, but actually I am a girl!"

THIRTY

Ajinkya had least expected such a severe shock. Kiran's eyes were dry like barren land. And Ajinkya's eyes started welling up. He caught Kiran in his arms tight and burst in tears. He said, "Don't worry. From here on, you will not work you'll only study! I will work to get a better future for you!"

Ajinkya wrapped her in the towel. He caught her arms. He picked her up on her feet. He walked with Kiran towards the couch. He made her sit on the couch. A cold drop fell from her eyes. It landed on Ajinkya's hand. He looked up. Her eyes are stilling flooding. Her eyes have turned red. He went on his knees. He wiped her eyes. He said, Kiran, now stop crying! Be brave! Forget what happened! Lets start life in a new manner again!

Kiran looked at him.

Omkar was standing behind the door. He heard the whole story. He entered the room. His eyes were also wet. He forwarded his hand to Kiran. He looked at Kiran and smiled.

He sat next to Kiran. Ajinkya smiled. He continued, I need to go out! I will be back soon!

Kiran caught his hand. Her throat has dried up. She opened her mouth but couldn't speak. She nodded her head. She asked him to stay with her. She didnt want to feel alone.

Ajinkya replied, Dont worry! I will be back soon. And Omkar is there with you! C'mon now smile!

Slowly a smile appeared on her face, but it was a fake one. Omkar went in the kitchen. Ajinkya hugged her. Omkar got a glass of water. She drank it like a dying man. Ajinkya whispered in Omkars ears, O m going out. I will be back soon!

Omkar exhaled air. He said, Hmm!

He said, "I want to be your best friend, Kiran!" Kiran looked at Ajinkya. He nodded his head. Kiran accepted his friendship! Ajinkya was happy.

Ajinkya said, "next month, I will fill your admission form. And promise me whenever you feel having a smoke or anything do tell me. We'll go together!"

Kiran nodded with a smile on her face. Kiran and Omkar hugged Ajinkya.

Omkar whispered, "I love you Kiran! I fell in love with you at first sight!"

Kiran replied, "I trust you!"

Omkar again said, "But what to say, you look awesome!

Kiran gave him a fight and said with a smile, "Quiet you naughty boy!"

Omkar replied, "Hassi toh ladki ka Ha hota hai!"

Kiran blushed and looked down.

Omkar said, "I told you I will make her laugh. See I kept my promise!"

Ajinkya happily agreed to it.

Ajinkya released Kiran from his arms. He got up. He walked to the door. He looked back at Omkar. Omkar looked at him. Something bothered Ajinkyas heart. Omkar went to him. He halted next to Ajinkya. Ajinkya took a breather. He warned Omkar in a calm voice, Don't try to do any mischief with her! Don't break her trust and my trust as well!

What? He reacted. What do you mean?

He paused for a while. Later he reacted, Don't you trust me?

I trust you! He kept quiet. He tapped Omkars right shoulder. He continued, But when a dream comes true, we fail to control our self and we do commit a mistake. She is in a shock. She trusts us. At this point it is difficult to control the devil. If you tell her to drop her towel, she might do so! And everything would go for a toss! So remember, this is your exam! I am checking your love and my trust! Best of luck!

He smiled. Omkar interlocked Ajinkyas wrist. He looked in his eyes and said, I wont let your trust break. Trust me!

Ajinkya tapped Omkars head and gave him a smile.

He walked down the stairs. He went in the parking. He reached his bike. He checked his right pant pocket for keys. He didnt find it. He checked each and every pocket. But he didnt find the keys. He recalled his memory. His bike keys were on the dining table, which he forgot to pick up.

He went to the lift. He called for the lift. In few seconds, the lift reached minus one. He opened the grill. He went in. He pressed second. The lift travelled up. It reached second floor. He opened the grill and walked out.

He stood in front of the main door of the house. He removed the keys of main door. He entered the keys in the computer-lock. He went in. The room was dark. The lights were turned off. He went in. As he walked in, he could hear movement in the bedroom. He went to the bedroom.

He saw the light have been turned off. Omkar was playing a movie on the computer. Kiran was busy watching the movie and laughing. Ajinkya gazed at them. Omkar noticed someones presence in the room. He looked at the door. He saw Ajinkya standing there. Ajinkya smiled and raised his bike-keys. Omkar smiled. Omkar nodded. Ajinkya whispered, Dont worry I trust you! Omkar couldnt hear Ajinkya. Ajinkya left. He guessed may be said, I trust you!

Ajinkya went down the stairs. He is happy. His trust has won over his doubts. He started his bike and he left. He drove the bike to the main street.

THIRTY-ONE

He went to the nearest kids store. He parked vehicle near the store on one stand. He looked at the store. He removed the keys and walked to the store. He looked at the clothes on display. He walked in. There are four sales persons. The shop-owner was sitting at the counter.

Ajinkya went to one of the sales person. He made his way through the rush.

He asked, Bhaiya show me some clothes!

He inquired, Bhaiya age?

Ajinkya replied, Ten! No Eleven!

He looked at the box kept in the shelf behind him. He again inquired, Boy or girl?

Ajinkya thought for a moment. The sales-person said to himself, what an idiot! He doesnt know for whom he has come to purchase clothes! Oh God!

Ajinkya replied, Girl! Show me dresses for regular usage!

Ok!

He displayed some clothes to him. Ajinkya selected clothes form different lots and patterns. He bought each and everything right from frocks, handkerchiefs, hair bands tops till innerwear as well. He swiped his card. He walked out with loads of bags.

He went to store next door. It's a stationery shop. He bought some ear rings, a necklace and an anklet. He bought a bracelet for Omkar. He paid them in cash as the amount was small. He walked to his bike. He hung the bags on the left handle.

He drove back to home. On his way, he saw a wada-pav stall. His mouth watered. He bought some hot wada-pav. In front of him saw a broken stall. Salim's tea stall! He crossed the road. He went near the broken stall. He didn't find anyone there. He came back to his bike. He started his bike and went to his office. He saw the place where the tea stall used to be was empty. He parked his biked. He crossed the busy traffic to go to the other side of the road. The tent had been dismantled. No one was there around it.

He looked around. He saw some people passing by.

He inquired Excuse me!

The other person in formals turned to him. He replied, Yes!

He pointed on the other side of the road. He continued, There was a tea stall there? Has it been shifted to a different place?

He replied, Oh! That was an illegal possession! The Government servicemen had come few days ago! They destroyed the tea stall and their tent!

Furious Ajinkya asked, So do you know where Javed went?

He replied, Javed? Oh that tall kid! No one knows where he went.

He left. Ajinkya went to the pan stall. He bought a cigarette from there. Suddenly an idea clicked his mind. He murmured, Let's look for Salim's house!

He inquired to pan stall vendor, hey do you know that tea stall vendor's house is?

He denied by nodding his head sideways. Ajinkya started his bike and left.

He reached home. He parked his bike. He climbed the stairs.

He murmured, Great! If I wouldn't have brought Kiran home then we might have lost her as well!

He murmured, Good one Ajinkya! He tapped his own shoulder.

He looked at the door. He looked at the name-plate. Jagdish Jadhav. He smiled.

He said, Dad, I know you are proud of me!

A drop of tear fell from his eye; it landed on his cheek. He wiped it by his small finger of his left hand. He transferred the carry bag on his left hand. He ran his right hand in his pocket. He removed the keys. He inserted the key in the lock. He unlocked the door. He went in.

He saw Kiran sitting on the couch. Omkar was sitting next to her. Both were watching movie Dil Chahta Hai on a movie channel. Kiran smiled to Ajinkya. Omkar got up. He took the carry bag from his hand. He kept it on the centre-table.

He picked one white packet. He removed some clothes. He picked up one frock from it. He gave it in Kiran's hand. Kiran blushed with joy. She hugged him. She went in to change. Ajinkya sat on the couch with Omkar. He gave Omkar the bracelet. Omkar was happy.

THIRTY-TWO

I Quit....Smoking!

It was a hot and dry bright Saturday. The rooster in the wall-clock crowed, "cock-a-doodle-doo". It's 4 in the evening. Kiran, dressed in red frock with small white spots, just returned home from her classes. She unlocked the doors with the key and walked in. She kept her bag in the bed room. She went in the kitchen and filled a glass of water and looked around. No one was home and there was peace all around. She drank and kept the glass back its place.

She went in all the rooms looking for Ajinkya. She murmured, "Today Ajinkya is on weekly off. Then where is he?"

Suddenly she heard a ringtone. She reached hall and saw Ajinkya's cell on the couch. She grabbed the phone. She read, "Krishna is calling, but where is Ajinkya?"

She walked to the door. She comprehended, "I am sure, he is upstairs! Let me check!"

She wore her slippers and latched the door. She climbed the ladders up. She entered the terrace. She saw Ajinkya and Rahul talking something and sharing a smoke. Ajinkya dressed in a three-fourth and a yellow T-shirt with a collar and Rahul dressed in blue T-shirt and white three-fourth. She halted and looked at them. Ajinkya left her presence and he turned towards her. He smiled. She approached her.

She gave him cell phone and stood beside them.

Rahul took a puff and said, "It had been long time, Neha was admitted to the hospital. You might require some financial support to bring up Kiran?"

He passed the cigarette to Ajinkya. Ajinkya took a puff and said, "Hmm!"

Rahul continued, "I can help you!"

Ajinkya interrupted, "Well, I don't require help. Thanks for that! Shree was paying most of medical expenses and I am paying for remaining and I can manage everything, don't worry!"

Rahul admired him and exhilarated, Ajinkya I am proud of you! I am proud to be your friend!

Thanks, Ajinkya replied with a smile.

Ajinkya passed the cigarette to Kiran. A strange expression popped up on Rahul's face and he questioned, "Ajinkya?"

Before he could complete, Ajinkya gave an expression as if he wanted to say, 'Don't be hyper! Cool!'

Kiran looked at Ajinkya. He looked into her eyes. Fear flashed through her eyes into Ajinkya's eyes. She took the cigarette. She took a puff.

Rahul was still confused. She took another puff. Suddenly her heart regretted, "Hey this is a bad habit. Leave it right way!"

She returned the cigarette back to Ajinkya. Kiran said, "Dad, let's quit smoking!"

Ajinkya remained stunted. This was the first instance when Kiran called him as "DAD" This was the most meaningful and emotional word for him. And this is not just a word, but a booster for him to a positive life!

He took the cigarette and crushed it below his shoe. Ajinkya said, "I QUIT! Chalo let's move down!"

They walked down the stairs. And thereafter Ajinkya and Kiran slowly and steadily left smoking!

THIRTY-THREE

Discovery of a celeb

Rahul was unhappy with the behaviour of his family. He was upset. Every week he had to go through a verbal war with his family on very small small, but important reasons!

He was tired and frustrated. He wanted to boycott his own house. He wished he to could go to a new place. A place where everyone would like him as he was; where he would not have to live his life as dictated by others! The people around him would support him and love him!

He didn't leave the house and go! Not because he couldn't dare, but because he was a responsible son!

But on a Saturday evening, the great wall of his patience shattered in pieces!

His mother was busy cooking in the kitchen and Omkar was in the hall busy watching cartoons, Rahul was fast asleep and was sweating; yet he had taken a blanket over!

The sun moved from East to high up in the sky indicating noon time; but Rahul was still deep asleep like the Mythological character 'Kumbhkaran'.

His mother came in the bedroom and gave him a call once then twice. An hour later, his sleep broke. He woke up. He rubbed his eyes. He looked around. The room was dark. The curtains were closed. He got up from the bed. He walked towards the wash basin with his lazy feet. His mother looked at him with her angry eyes. She was busy cutting vegetables. He stood in front of the wash-basin. He stretched his eyes to open them wide. He turned the tap and splashed water on his face. The water was hot. "Oops! It's hot!"

His mother commented, "Omkar give your brother cold water from the fridge to wash his face!"

Omkar stood up and peeped into the kitchen. He glanced at her with a crooked face. Rahul looked at his mother. He said to himself, "She has started! I have just got up! Please God! I'm tired!"

Mother shouted, "get up Omkar! Give him chilled water!"

Omkar said, “Oh God! Both have started again!”

He kept the remote on the dining table. He went to the kitchen. He opened the fridge door. He removed a chilled bottle. He closed the door. He gave the bottle to his brother. Rahul felt insulted. He refused taking the bottle. He washed his face. Omkar kept the bottle in the fridge and went back in the hall. He sat on the chair. He resumed watching television.

Rahul brushed his teeth. He went back in the bedroom. He took his towel. He went in the washroom.

Omkar murmured, “I think I might have to leave, they will start again! Let’s go to Ajinkya bhaiya’s house!”

He stood up. He heard the water falling from the shower. He thought, “I think bhaiya has gone for a bath! Thank God! I am tired of this quarrel!”

Sometime later his mother went near the washroom and banged the door. She came back to the kitchen. The sound of water falling from the shower stopped. He opened the door. He removed his face out with soap all around. He looked around with narrowed eyes.

She said, “Turn the tap off! Today the Municipal Corporation will not release water! Don’t waste water!”

He quietly went in. He closed the door. He turned the tap off. Around fifteen minutes later, he came out wearing a brown vest and black pyjamas and a towel across his neck. Water dripped from his hair. He went to the bedroom and wiped his head.

His mother came out of the kitchen. She looked down. She took a piece of cloth and she wiped the place. She didn't say anything to Rahul.

Rahul felt better after the bath. He combed his hair. He opened the box kept below his pillow. He removed his specs and wore them. He went into the hall. He emptied half the bottle of water. He sat on the chair just behind Omkar. He looked at the Television. He was bored watching cartoon. He raised his hand towards Omkar.

Rahul asked "Omkar give me the remote! Let me check what is going on the other channels!"

Omkar refused.

Rahul asked him again calmly. Omkar acted as if he didn't hear him. Rahul got up and he pulled the remote from Omkar's hand. He switched to ESPN. English Premier League was on.

Omkar shouted, "Mummy!" She stood on her toe to see what was wrong! Omkar looked at his mother. He said, "Mumma see he pulled the remote from my hand!"

Mother taunted, "Let him watch Omkar! He is earning so he is the boss! He gets up like the King! We are his servants!"

Rahul became red. He wrapped the remote tight in his right palm.

She continued "He wants things as per his time! We should adjust with his schedule! We are slaves!"

He banged the remote on the floor with force. The body of the remote fell in two different directions.

She raised her voice, "He earns but he doesn't know the price of each paisa!"

He bit his lips between his teeth. He looked at his mother with anger. But he couldn't speak anything as his stomach cried for food. He kept quiet.

She said, "Don't show me attitude! I work here like a slave for you people! And only then you get two times food!"

Suddenly a knock was heard at the door. Omkar opened the door. The lady living a floor below them was standing at the door. She asked, "Did someone fall?"

Mother pointed towards Rahul and said, "No he banged the remote on the floor!"

Omkar interrupted, "Mumma what are you doing! Let the family matter be between the four walls!"

She said, "No it's his mistake because of which the wife of our society's chairman has come upstairs!"

She taunted Rahul with attitude, "Don't you know how to live in a society! This is not a slum!"

She indirectly passed a taunt onto Rahul, "Let it be! This generation does not have manners to behave in a house. They should leave their house and live separately! Especially call center people!"

Rahul went in. He sat down on the bed. Anger flashed through his eyes. Each and every word pierced his heart, his ego, his pride! He picked a travel bag. He started filling his clothes. He could still hear the ladies speaking at the door. Omkar went downstairs to the parking.

Twenty minutes later, he came up. He saw Rahul had packed his bag. He was filling his documents in a file. Shock struck his brain. He couldn't understand what he was doing!

He inquired, "Bhaiya why are you packing the bag?"

"I am leaving this house!"

"What?"

He went in the kitchen.

"Mumma, bhaiya is packing his bag. Stop him!"

"It needs courage to leave the house!"

Rahul could hear her sharp comments.

Omkar ran downstairs. He ran to Ajinkya's house. He banged the door rapidly. Kiran opened the door. He looked at Kiran. She was wearing a pair of blue jeans and a black top. Ajinkya was sitting on the couch and reading newspaper. He looked at Omkar. Omkar's eyes flooded. A streak of tears ran over his red cheeks. Ajinkya got up. He threw the newspaper aside. And he ran to Omkar. Omkar hugged Ajinkya. He was crying without voice. Ajinkya ran his palm on his wet hair. Omkar narrated to him the whole story.

Ajinkya was shocked. He ran down the stairs. Omkar sat on the couch. Kiran went into the kitchen and she brought a glass of chilled water. He was feeling so thirsty that he drank the glass of chilled water in one sip.

Ajinkya went upstairs to Rahul's house. The door was open. He went in. Rahul was sitting on the chair and wearing his socks. One Travel bag and one shoulder bag were kept on the floor in front of him. He was ready to leave the house.

Ajinkya pulled a chair next to him. He sat on the chair. He poured a glass of water from the jug. He drank it. He looked at Rahul. Rahul was trying to hide his face. Ajinkya kept the empty glass on the table. Rahul wore his shoes. He got up. He pulled the bags over his shoulder. He walked down the stairs. Ajinkya followed him.

Rahul looked back. He did not utter a word. His heart was full. His brain froze. He was not sure what he was doing. They reached the parking. He walked towards his bike. He kept the bags on the back seat. He removed a rope to pack them. Ajinkya pulled off the bags from the seat.

Rahul said in a disappointed voice, “What happened?”

“Where are you going?”

“Don’t know?”

“Why are you going?”

“I am tired! I don’t want to live here!” He said aggressively.

“So!”

“So?” he questioned. “Enough is enough!! For whom am I working? For them right!” he shouted. Ajinkya sat on his bike. “For whom am I working a night shift?? For them right! And what am I getting in return?? I don’t have my own identity!”

“So what want do you want to do?”

“I want to go to Mumbai!”

“Why?”

“I want to become a script-writer! I have done couple of plays here and a certified course of it!”

“So why didn’t you go?”

"They didn't want me to do that!"

"And then why did you join call center?"

"Because, because they wanted me to earn money! I felt that I can become their good son who will always take..." He broke into tears. Ajinkya got up. He hugged him. A drop of tear fell from Ajinkya's eyes. He wiped his eyes. He caught him tight. He said, "Let's go home!" He denied by nodding his head.

"Bachha, to my house! Let's move!"

They walked towards Ajinkya's house. Rahul wiped his eyes. Rahul sat on the couch. Kiran switched on the fan. Rahul tried to avoid Omkar. He said to himself, "Bhaiya is angry! I should not speak with him right now!"

He went to Ajinkya. He looked down. He said, "Thank you Bhaiya!"

Ajinkya pulled his face up. A tear drop fell on Ajinkya's thumb.

Ajinkya said, "Hey!" He wiped his eyes. Ajinkya picked Omkar up and took him to the bedroom. He hugged Omkar. Omkar said, "Thank you!"

Ajinkya looked in eyes and said, "Stop crying! I am your best friend?"

"Love you brother!"

They went in the hall. Rahul was sitting on the couch along with his heavy stress crown on his head!

Omkar said, "Bhaiya, do something? There is tension in the room!"

"As you say sir!" Ajinkya replied to Omkar.

"So friends lets cook chicken together!"

Rahul looked at Ajinkya's smiling face.

"But I don't know to cook!" replied Rahul.

"Doesn't matter! Dum biryani is your favourite, right!"

Rahul looked at the floor.

Ajinkya said, "You can cut the vegetables and enjoy it in lunch!"

Rahul nodded his head.

"So get up guys! Let's move! Chalo, Chalo, chalo!"

They all rushed in the kitchen and left the television set switched on. Omkar opened the fridge. He removed the tray of chicken from the freezer. He went in the kitchen. Kiran removed the vegetable tray, removed the required vegetables and kept the tray back in the fridge and closed it.

They worked together and chopped the vegetables. Rahul and Ajinkya recollected the nuisance and stupidity laughed they did in their childhood! Those incidences made everyone laugh.

They laughed and cried as well! The Bloody onions made everyone cry; except Ajinkya. Well, why? Because he did not cut onions!

They served Dum biryani. They enjoyed it so much that they didn't realize when the clock reached 3 o'clock. After lunch everyone went deep asleep.

THIRTY-FOUR

It was six in the evening. The cock from within the clock came out and crowed. It broke Omkar's sleep. He opened his eyes. He rubbed his eyes with his fingers. He looked around. He saw Kiran sleeping next to him on the bed. The Snakes and ladder board was kept below her head. The coins and dice were lying on the bed. He recalled they were playing snake and ladder, but couldn't remember when they went to sleep!

He got up. He stretched his hands. He yawned. He looked back at Kiran. Kiran was sleeping peacefully. His eyes were caught by her lips. Her lips were thin but looked sweet.

He went back on the bed. He bent towards Kiran. He went near her. His lips turned dry. He took a deep breath. His heart started beating fast. He opened his lips. He went close to kiss her. It felt like she was awake, but the only thing he wanted him to kiss her. Suddenly, a big bang was heard!

Kiran opened her eyes. Omkar pushed himself far away from her. Kiran got up and ran into the hall. She saw Rahul trying to get up. He slipped on the floor. It had hurted his elbow and knees. He got up.

"Oops!" he cried. "My knees! Oh God!"

Kiran gave her hand to Rahul. Rahul got up with her support.

He thanked her. "No thanks bhaiya!" she replied.

Omkar came in the hall. Ajinkya was still sleeping on the couch peacefully.

Kiran said, "Omkar wake Ajinkya bhaiya!"

Omkar replied, "Yes!"

He walked towards the couch. Rahul said, "Let it be Omkar! Let him sleep! I have seen him sleeping peacefully after many months! Otherwise he keeps on running everywhere. Let him sleep!"

Kiran said, "But bhaiya, it's almost 6:15!"

Rahul replied, "Fine! Wake him up ten minutes later!"

He looked at Ajinkya. He went to the washroom.

Around 6:45 PM. Ajinkya woke up. The saliva ran from his mouth to his hand. His wrist had become sticky. He opened his eyes. He looked around. He saw Kiran and Omkar sitting on the floor and watching a Hindi movie channel. The room was dark.

He stressed his eyes to look at the time. But he could not read it. He got up. He walked to the washroom. A while later, he walked out. He saw Rahul cutting vegetables. He went in the kitchen.

"What are you doing Rahul?"

"Cutting vegetables for dinner!"

"So what have you planned to make tonight?"

"Not sure! Let's see!" Ajinkya said while removing the utensils.

"Did you have tea?" Ajinkya inquired.

"Yes Kiran had given it to me!"

"Ok! Would you like to have more?"

"No! I just need a break!"

Ajinkya looked at him. "I am going to the balcony!" Rahul said.

He kept the knife and the chopped vegetables in the tray. He picked it up and kept it on the platform. He went in the balcony. Ajinkya started the burner. Ajinkya noticed the lines of stress on his face.

Rahul removed the cigarette packet from his pocket, took a cigarette and lit it. He felt better. Suddenly, Kiran and Omkar came into the balcony. He did not crush the cigarette. He looked at them. They stood quietly next to him.

Omkar caught Rahul's hand. He said in a soft voice, "I am sorry bhaiya!"

Rahul kept quiet. He looked at him. He hugged Omkar near his chest. Kiran went in the kitchen to see Ajinkya.

Rahul crushed the cigarette on his palm. He kissed Omkar's forehead. They went into the hall. He switched on the television. He sat on the couch. Omkar sat on his lap. Rahul hugged him. A tear dropped from Rahul's eyes. He wiped his eyes. Omkar looked back. He asked, "What happened? Why are you crying?"

He answered, "No! My eyes are paining!"

Omkar caught his palm firmly. Rahul felt better.

The clock shouted. Kiran looked at the wall clock. Nine!

"Dinner is ready!" said Ajinkya.

Rahul looked at him.

Ajinkya said, "Tomorrow let's go for a picnic!"

Omkar reacted, "That's great!"

Kiran asked, "But where?"

Ajinkya replied, "To a water resort nearby!"

Omkar reacted with joy, "So let's pack our bags!"

Kiran said, "But now let's have dinner!"

"Ok!" replied Ajinkya with a smile. "Get the plates, and Omkar bring four spoons!"

Kiran and Omkar rushed in the kitchen. Ajinkya and Omkar served dinner. Everyone sat and started the dinner.

Ajinkya said, "So script writer, write a story by tomorrow! We would like to hear it!"

Rahul stopped and looked at Ajinkya. Omkar and Kiran said, "Yes bhaiya! Yes!"

Rahul smiled and said, "That's fine!"

Ajinkya said, "So be ready! Tomorrow is your exam before we leave from here! Morning six!"

Omkar inquired, "Bhaiya, is Pooja coming with us?"

Kiran looked at Ajinkya. Ajinkya answered, "I am not in touch with her! I think she will not be with us!"

Rahul inquired, "Who is Pooja?"

Ajinkya replied, "She is my school friend and a doctor.."

Omkar interrupted, "Brother I will tell you later! First, focus on your work!"

He said to Ajinkya, "I will go and invite her!" He got up. He looked at Rahul and said, "Let's move bhaiya!"

"But where are we going? Do you know her address?" he questioned.

Ajinkya answered, "Her clinic is in the main bazaar!" He looked at the time. Ya, it will be open, now as well!"

"Ok!" replied Rahul in a calm voice.

Rahul picked the bike keys. They both left.

They ran down the stairs. He started the bike. Omkar sat on the back seat and they left.

"So, who is Pooja?"

Omkar blushed. Rahul looked in the mirror and said, "Why are you blushing?"

"She is Ajinkya's school-mate. I feel like she loves Ajinkya!"

Rahul stopped the bike with shock and replied, "What! Are you serious?"

"Yes! I have seen the shine in her eyes!"

"Wow!" He kick started his bike again. "I want to meet her! Let's move!"

THIRTY-FIVE

Rahul spent long hours to think about a good concept. A concept which would be very different, and that would impress everyone. His talent would be on test tomorrow. Everyone went to sleep around 11 PM. He went to sleep, but he could not sleep. He changed his sleeping position, but still sleep did not knock him out. He was tired. He had lost his peace. He got up and sat on the bed.

He alone was awake in the dark room. He scratched his head. He went in the balcony for a walk. Later he went in the hall. He sat on the couch. He switched on the television. He lowered down the volume. He swapped channels.

He murmured, "What should I write?"

He grabbed a pen and paper. He scribbled something in the dark. Sometime later, he went to deep asleep. He slept late, around 3 AM. The television remained on.

The Sun woke up at 5:40 am. He loves to see and listen to talented people. He was eager to listen to Rahul's story! He stretched his arms as far he could. He pushed the cloud behind. He showered his shine all around.

Everyone got up in a hurry. Ajinkya came in the hall. He switched off the television.

One by one, everyone got ready to leave. Omkar came in the hall. He opened the windows. The wind bashed into the room and bashed Rahul.

Omkar yawned and said, "Bhaiya, get up!"

He shook his arms. Rahul stressed his eyes to open them. The wind blew into his eyes. He closed and rubbed them. He said, "What happened?"

Omkar yawned. He said, "Get ready! We have to leave! Wake up fast!"

He replied, "Yes!"

He changed his sleeping position to the other side. Omkar went to the washroom. The wind took a small run-up. He came with full speed in the room. The cold breeze ran over Rahul. Rahul shivered and got up.

“It’s too cold!” he said.

Suddenly a knock was heard on the door.

“Who has come at this time?”

He looked at the wall clock. “It’s just 7? Uff!” Rahul murmured.

Omkar came into the hall. He kept the blanket on the couch. He opened the door. Dr. Pooja had come to their door.

“Hi!” she said. She came in. Rahul stood up in hurry. He pushed his blanket on the couch.

“Come in! Have a seat!”

She sat on the couch. Rahul went in to get ready. He went in the washroom. Ajinkya was getting ready. He had already packed his bag. He came in the hall.

“Omkar have you packed you bag?” He said.

Omkar replied “Yes I have!”

Ajinkya felt that someone was there. He turned and said, “Hi! Good Morning! How are you?”

“I am fine!” she replied. Ajinkya questioned, “Where were you these days?”

She replied “I was very busy !”

Omkar and Kiran stared at them.

Ajinkya again questioned “You didn’t answer my phone calls as well!”

She apologized “I am sorry!”

Omkar murmured “They have so much formality!”

Ajinkya inquired, “Omkar did you had something?”

“No! I did not!” Omkar replied.

He went in.

By 7:30, everyone was ready to leave. They had breakfast together.

Ajinkya went downstairs. Everyone walked down and they left.

THIRTY-SIX

They had booked a car to a private transport agency. Ajinkya and Rahul sat in front. Omkar and Kiran sat behind with Pooja.

"So have you written the story?" Ajinkya inquired.

"Yes bhaiya?" inquired Kiran and Omkar.

"Hmm! Yes, I have written it!" Rahul replied.

"So what are you waiting for?" Ajinkya said.

"Here?" Rahul questioned with shock.

"Yes! Start!" Pooja said.

"Fine!" He took a deep breath and pushed his stress out.

"This story is a poor struggling singer who falls in love with a rich girl."

Omkar murmured, "Hmm!"

"But her parents deny their relationship and their ways parted in different directions! She gets married to a rich guy! He gets addicted to alcohol! But one day he meets an accident! The person who was driving is found to be his old friend! He brings the struggling singer in Bollywood! Now he is a Rock star! Suddenly one day he meets his old love!"

Pooja looked at Ajinkya who looked like a good listener! His eyes were closed, but Kiran and Omkar noticed the shine on her face.

Rahul continued, "But they are now only friends! Soon they become good friends. They started meeting up. And this messed the couple's married life! Soon the girl brought this into Rockstar's notice. He met the husband and tried explaining. But the husband was husband, and he was adamant! Rock star started getting calls from underworld for money. He refused. He went on his world performance tour. He came back. He threw a success party and asked both of them to come! The underworld don gave supari to kill the rock star in this party. He is hit. He gets the couple back together! Later the rockstar's soul comes and takes to past. And finally its revealed that rockstar was the don himself!"

"Oh!" Kiran reacted. Pooja remains numb.

Omkar reacted, "She! What type of story is this?"

Ajinkya reacted, "This story is perfect! It has emotions! Awesome dude!"

"Good!" Pooja said and clapped as Ajinkya liked it and concept was different as well.

"Thank you!" Rahul replied with smile.

They reached the water-park. Ajinkya stopped the car.

"So here we are!" Ajinkya announced.

"Wow!" Kiran said.

Let's move!" Omkar said.

"Let's move!" he said to Pooja.

THIRTY-SEVEN

They went in. They had their lunch. They then went to change. Soon, everyone got down into the water.

"So where were you these days?" Ajinkya questioned.

"Well I was busy in my work!" Pooja replied.

"You forgot your friend!" Ajinkya complained.

"I am sorry!" said Pooja.

Sometime later, Ajinkya came out of the water. He sat on the wooden chair kept in front of the swimming pool. Rahul followed him and sat on the adjacent chair. Ajinkya glanced at Pooja.

"So do you love Pooja?" Rahul inquired.

He paused and then answered "No!"

"Then why are you staring at her?" Rahul counter-attacked.

"Oh! I am staring at Kiran! After many days I have seen her smiling!" Ajinkya answered.

Rahul remained numb. Ajinkya looked at Rahul.

"Well! Don't leave the company in one day! Keep a backup!" Ajinkya advised. Rahul looked at him.

"Understand one thing! It's not assured that you will go there and immediately you will get your dream job!"

"So?" Rahul inquired.

"So in case you are in need of money you can work in a BPO!" Ajinkya continued.

"You are right!" Rahul said.

"And that's the only reason I am asking you to serve one month notice-period!" Ajinkya said.

"Ok I will do so! Don't worry!" Rahul said and remained silent. A teardrop came out of his eyes.

“Thanks for being my friend!” Rahul said.

“Hey!” Ajinkya consoled him and hugged him. “You are very good!” Rahul said.

Ajinkya smiled. Rahul said, “Start being a bit selfish!”

THIRTY-EIGHT

It's Sunday morning. Everyone is back from the picnic spot last night. Pooja has gone to her house. Everyone is tired and deep asleep.

Suddenly Ajinkya's phone buzzed. He picked the phone kept below his pillow. He answered, "Yes!"

The person on the other end said, "Ajinkya?"

"Hmm! Yes!" Ajinkya replied in a sleepy tone.

"Hi! How are you?" from the other said.

Fine!" He yawned, "Sorry! Who is it?"

"Hey! I am Shri!" from the other end.

He opened his eyes with surprise. He looked at the cell phone screen. He checked the number reflecting on his screen.

"Yes, this is his number!" he murmured.

"Are you there?" Shri inquired.

"Yes, I am! What happen?" Ajinkya replied.

"I need to meet you!" Shri said.

"Come home!" Ajinkya replied.

"No something very personal!" Shri replied.

"Fine! Mac D in Camp!" Ajinkya said.

"That's fine, at 1!" Shri replied.

Ajinkya looked at his watch. Last night, he was so tired that he had not changed before going off to sleep.

He murmured again, "It's Eleven thirty!"

He said, "Fine! I will be there!"

He disconnected the call. He got up. He kept the cell phone on the bed. He went for shower.

He reached at Mac Donald's at 1. He sat on the first table. Shri has yet not arrived at the Mac D. He murmured "Maybe, he is late!"

He ordered for a soup. He looked at the door. Shree arrived. He sat. The waiter served soup. Ajinkya took a sip. Shree said, "I need to speak with you!"

"Yes!" Ajinkya said.

Shri took a sip. He inquired "Have you planned anything about your marriage?"

He paused.

He continued "Pooja loves you right!"

Ajinkya glanced at him.

He continued, "So why don't you forget Neha?"

Ajinkya crumpled the tissue kept on the table. He said, "Why?"

Shree kept quiet. He looked at Ajinkya.

"You are stuck in your past! She is your past and Pooja is your present. Kiran is a girl. A mother can take better care of her! Understand the gravity of your life! This is the necessity of the situation."

"Ok! I will think about it!"

He got up. He went to the bill counter. He paid the bill. He looked back at Shree. Ajinkya felt shameful. He murmured, "Yes he is right!"

He walked out. He started his bike and left. He went back home. He started the computer. He went in Start, Programs, FIFA. He played but he was mentally absent. He was speaking with his own self.

"Why am I not selfish? Why am I like this? I care for others? I have to live for myself so that I do well for others!"

Everyone noticed that Ajinkya was disturbed. He lost the match by 6-0.

Ajinkya sat on the bed. He wrote some lines in his diary.

I am tense today!

Why am I like this? I don't know!

I care for everyone in this world except, except myself! Why?

This same question arose today as well! Shree picked it up!

Everyone has realized I am a jerk!

What next is on my way? God knows! Hmm!

Gud bye! And gud night to myself!

He closed the dairy. He fell back. He closed his eyes. He was very tired due to the conflict in his mind. He fell asleep.

THIRTY-NINE

Mr. Chaubey and Ajinkya reached the office early. They sat at their workstation and started checking the mails.

About ten minutes later, the agents came in. Everyone gathered near Mr. Chaubey's port. Rahul also arrived. Mr. Chaubey got busy checking something in the excel-sheet.

Ajinkya asked, "So guys how are you all?"

"Fine sir!" the crowd replied.

Ajinkya inquired "How was everyone's weekend?"

The crowd replied "Good!"

He again inquired "Hope no one is drunk today!"

The crowd replied "No!"

Krishna came in. He stood between the other agents.

Ajinkya said "So get back to work! Need to have an early start!"

The crowd replied "Yes sir!"

Everyone started moving to their respective ports. Krishna also moved.

Ajinkya said "Stop Krishna!" He halted.

Ajinkya questioned "Why are you late?"

He turned towards Ajinkya. Mr. Chaubey looked at Krishna.

Mr. Chaubey asked "Where is your I-card?"

He murmured "Oops!"

He scratched his head. He pulled his I-card from the back pocket of his pant.

Ajinkya said "I need to speak with you! Move to the conference room!"

He quietly moved. Ajinkya shouted, "Guys start collections! Start makes a difference!"

He left the floor. He went in the conference room. He saw Krishna resting on the chair.

"So what wrong?" Ajinkya inquired in a calm.

He looked at him. He remained silent.

"Why is your performance down?" Ajinkya again questioned with a raising voice.

He remained silent. "Speak up!"

After a pause Ajinkya asked "And why have you still not worn in your I-card?"

Krishna replied "I don't want to wear it!"

Ajinkya inquired "Why?"

He agitated "I feel uncomfortable!"

Ajinkya burst out on him. He said "You know what? You are not serious with your job! You are at the wrong place! You should put your papers down!"

Krishna inquired with shock "What?"

Ajinkya said "This job is giving you your bread and butter! And you feel insulted to put the I-card around your neck! Put down your papers or else work here for free! Then I would not ask to wear the I-card around your neck!"

"Hmm!" he taunted.

Ajinkya said "This job has given me an opportunity to walk with pride and respect!"

Krishna taunted again "Look who is speaking!"

Ajinkya reacted "What?"

Krishna said "You can only show off that you are working for others, but you think I am fool? I can see love in your eyes for Pooja! But you still deny it!"

He interrupted with anger "Yes I love her, but this is not the time to talk about love! You idiots are wasting money on liquor! Even if you take a single needy person's responsibility upon yourself, you will feel awesome! But you will not understand that!"

He calmed down. He sat on the chair. He took a deep breath. He got up.

Ajinkya said with a calm voice "This is not your job! You are in a wrong field! Think once more! Put your papers down! I don't want my manager to ask you to do that!"

He walked to the door. He opened the door and looked back.

Ajinkya said "Best of luck for your future!"

He moved out on the floor. He wiped his moist eyes.

He went to his port where Mr. Chaubey was sitting. He looked at him. He then looked on the screen of his laptop.

"What happened, Ajinkya?"

He replied with a calm voice, "I have asked him to put down his papers!"

He looked at Ajinkya's serious face.

"So this is a bad day for you!" Mr. Chaubey said.

"Hmm!"

"You have lost one teammate today and another one is serving notice period to the company!" Mr. Chaubey said.

"Yes!" Ajinkya replied.

"Your team is in danger now!" Mr. Chaubey said.

"I will cope up sir! If required I will log in! But I will not let you down!" Ajinkya replied with confidence.

FORTY

The next morning Ajinkya went to Dr. Pooja's clinic. She was busy reading a newspaper in her cabin. He knocked at the door. "Excuse me!"

She looked up at the door. She smiled. She folded the newspaper and kept it aside.

"Hi!"

"Hi!" Ajinkya replied.

"Come in!"

He walked in. He smiled.

"Have a seat!"

He sat. She picked up the newspaper. He looked at her. She started reading the newspaper. He started playing with the colourful paper weight.

Ajinkya waited for her to look at him to begin the topic. The his heart said, "No! speak up!"

He replied "No! I am scared!"

Ajinkya's phone buzzed. He removed his cell phone. He answered it, "Yes!" From the other end the person said, "Hello! Ajinkya?"

"Yes speaking!"

From the other end "I have submitted the adoption documents!"

"Thank you!" he replied with smile. Ajinkya said "Next week we need to go and get an admission for.. for Kiran!"

"Ok! Adoption procedure will take one year's time!"

Ajinkya hung up the phone. He smiled. Dr. Pooja was watching him from the corner of her eyes.

He stopped rotating the paper weight. He said "Pooja I need to speak with you!"

She was still busy reading newspaper. He said, "Yes!"

"I know why you were not coming to my house these days!"

She looked up.

Ajinkya continued "But I need tell you that I.."

She closed the newspaper. She looked up without making eye contact.

"I love you!" he said.

She was stunned. She first glanced at him, and later she smiled.

"I cannot believe it!" she said.

"I am telling you the truth!" he replied.

She became happy. A teardrop fell from her eyes. He took the droplet on his finger tip. He took it in front of her. He said, "Will you marry me?"

"Yes!" she blushed and said. She brought her eyes in contact with his eyes. He sucked the drop.

FORTY-ONE

10th June 2005

It's a Sunday. That's exciting for working people and kids. It's a holiday. For kids, this is the last day of holidays to enjoy. From tomorrow regular school will be in picture.

Tomorrow Kiran will go back to school. She is highly excited. Her hard work had been rewarded by God!

Yesterday, Ajinkya, Pooja and Kiran were awake till late night. They covered the school books in brown paper. Though they were awake till late night, they got up early.

It's 9 AM. Pooja has prepared special lemon grass tea. Kiran was sitting on the couch next to Ajinkya. Both are still in their night suits. They were busy reading the heavy supplements of Sunday Times. Kiran was trying to read the big difficult sentences.

Pooja came in the hall with a tray in her hand. There were three china cups with tea. She kept the tray on the centre table. She sat on the couch.

She looked at Ajinkya and Kiran. They were still busy reading the newspaper.

She said, "Keep the newspaper aside! Have your tea!"

She picked her cup. She took a sip.

The essence of lemon grass tea tickled their nose.

Ajinkya praised, "Wow! It smells good! It's Lemon grass tea!"

Ajinkya kept the newspaper to his left. Kiran followed him.

Kiran said, "Yes!"

They picked their cups. They took a sip.

Kiran praised, "It's really good! Teach me as well!"

Pooja said, "Yes! But now you have to study, Ok!"

Kiran replied "Hmm!"

Kiran smiled and looked at Ajinkya. She said, "Thank You, AJ!"

Ajinkya looked at her. He gave a strange look and inquired, "What is AJ?"

Pooja took another sip.

Kiran replied, "Dad, Ajinkya Jadhav! You are my inspiration!"

Ajinkya interrupted her, "Hey! That's your hard work! I have done nothing!"

Pooja said, "Last two weeks, we have completed the revision of Fourth standard!"

Kiran said, "Yes!"

Ajinkya inquired, "So, do you have any doubts?"

Kiran replied with a smile, "No doubts!"

Ajinkya took a sip. He said, "Kiran you are going to step into a new world where you will find many new friends. Everyone will be unknown to you. Don't have blind faith or trust on anyone! Take time to judge and understand them! Choose good friends! And the most important thing is to stop fearing!"

Kiran replied, "Hmm!"

Ajinkya continued, "Fear only when you are wrong! Immediately apologize! You will win everyone's trust!"

Kiran said, "Yes!"

Ajinkya took a deep breath and continued, "You might think I am giving you a lecture! But later you will realize that I am correct!"

Kiran said, "Don't worry! I am taking it positively!"

Ajinkya continued, "And last but not the least enjoy the life, because you might not get it again!"

Pooja nodded her head. Kiran thought about her past and gave a smile.

FORTY-TWO

Monday morning. The sun was dim. He was looking down on the earth through the grey clouds. Maybe he was tired of his routine life. So the clouds started covering him. Everyone started expecting rain, but the monsoon clouds had yet not arrived! They were stuck in traffic due to the black gases coming from the chimneys!

Today it's the First Day of School! Kids were excited. They would meet their friends and teachers after two months.

Ajinkya had come to drop Kiran to her school on his bike. He had to go somewhere urgently. Kiran steps down from the back seat. She was wearing a uniform and a hair band around her head. She had a school bag on her shoulder and a Tiffin bag in her hand. She stood in front of Ajinkya. She looked at the school building. It's a three storey Cream coloured building. He said, "Kiran, today I'm in hurry! But next time I will come with you, till your classroom, to drop you! Sorry for today! If you need anything, ask Omkar! He is also completing schooling here!"

Kiran said, "That's fine! I will go! Don't worry!"

He raised his hand and tapped her shoulder. He shifted the gear and left. She turned towards the school.

Students of different ages were walking to their classroom. Some children were accompanied by their parents; some had come by public and school transport; students who live nearby had come walking.

A decorated big black gate welcomed the students. A security guard stood next to it; there was a big ground and in the middle, the school building.

She climbed the stairs of the school building. There were different offices like school office, sports office, extra-curriculum office, and library and staff room at the ground floor. She saw a peon. She walked to him.

She said, "Uncle where is the Fifth standard classroom?"

He said, "Second floor Third classroom on the left from these stairs!"

She smiled and said, "Thank you Uncle!"

She climbed the stairs to go to the first floor. She saw that each classroom had its individual notice-board. She climbed up to the second floor. She admired the interior of the building and corridors. It seemed to be A British raj school! Everything was neat and tidy. There was a dustbin at every corner.

She took a left. She reached the third classroom. She looked up. A green name plate is hanging high up. On it, it was printed, 'Std. 5Th Div A'

She walked in. There were four rows. The classroom was beautifully decorated with last year's chart and clean shiny blackboard. Two speakers were fixed opposite each other in the class. There was a wooden table for the teacher and a chair as well. She looked for a place to sit.

There was a vacant place on the third bench of the second row. A boy was sitting there. She walked ahead. Some of them noticed her later. For them, she was new and unknown. She reached the third bench. She stopped.

The boy was busy scribbling on the bench with a compass. He was writing his name. She asked him, "Can I sit here?"

He looked up. He looked at her from top to bottom. She inquired again, "Can I sit here?"

He said, "Uh? Yes!"

She kept her school bag on the bench and Tiffin bag below it. She sat on the desk. He raised his hand in front. He said, "I am Prashant Bhurewar!"

He wanted to shake hands with her. She looked at him. She looked at the black-board. She said, "I am Kiran!"

She did not shake hand with him. He pulled his hand back.

The bell rang and the students of 5th grade started moving down.

Suddenly, a thunder storm blinked in the sky. Today Varun dev blessed everyone with the first monsoon rain!

"Welcome students, back to school! It's raining out! Students are asked to go to their respective classes."

Students rushed back in the classroom. A minute later the class teacher came. She was dressed up in a yellow colour sari. Everyone got up and wished her, "Good morning teacher!"

She replied with a smile, "Good morning everyone!"

She kept her pouch on her table. She walked to the students.

She said, "Students join your hands! Let's start the prayer!"

She joined her hands and closed her eyes. Everyone followed her.

FORTY-THREE

Mathematics is a Game!

The bell rang. Prashant said, "It's Mathematics period now. I hate it!"

Professor Sutar with a big boil on his head walked in. Everyone got up and wished him. He replied, "Good morning! Sit down! How was everyone's vacation?"

Everyone sat down. Prashant commented, "Everyone is asking the same question since morning! Vacation was better! At least it was not boring!"

Kiran looked at him.

Professor Sutar continued, "Ok! Let's revise some formulae!"

So saying, he picked a piece of chalk from the table. He walked to the blackboard. He started writing some problems. He turned to the students. He commanded, "Tell me the steps to solve these problems!"

He looked at the class. No one was ready to get up and answer. A fair boy with short height stood up. He said, "Sir, I will answer the first question!"

Professor replied, "Good!"

Prashant murmured, "He is the rank one of the class, Rohit! We call him champu!"

Kiran gave him an angry look. Prashant looked at her and said, "Well look at his hair!"

Professor said, "Now the last problem!"

The whole class looked tense. Professor said, "Ok! No one then I will pick someone to solve it!"

He pointed at the third bench of the second row. Prashant looked at his finger. It is directed to him. Prashant commented, "Oh shit! Not me, please God!"

He covered his face with his hands. Professor said, "You the girl at the third bench!"

Kiran stood up. Prashant took a deep breath and said, "Thank God! But Kiran it's a difficult question!"

Kiran replied, "Fine!"

Kiran looked at the blackboard. She read the question, "Ramu took a loan of Rs. 50,000 for 3 years on half yearly interest of 7.5, then what will be the interest he has to pay?"

She looked at Professor. She closed her eyes and took a deep breath. She said, "It is simple. We need to apply Formula P X R X N / 100."

Professor smiled. He said, "Ok! It's difficult! You can come here and solve it!"

Kiran said, "Yes sir! But I want to solve it verbally!"

Prashant said, "Are you mad?"

Kiran replied to him, "You should be quiet!"

She closed her eyes and started calculating.

Kiran continued, "P is equal to 50,000 and R is 7.5 and N is 3. Now the answer will be!"

The whole class looked at her with an emotionless faces.

She said, "So the total will be around Rs. 1125000 and divided by 100."

She opened her eyes. Her eyes became big in size with confidence. She said, "The total interest comes to Rs. 11250!"

Prashant dropped his jaws down and blinked his eyes. Professor Sutar clapped. Everyone followed him. Kiran smiled. Professor Sutar smiled and said, "What is your name?"

She replied, "Kiran! Kiran Kulkarni!"

He said, "Good, good! You can sit down!"

She sat back on the bench. The school bell rang. Prashant inquired, "How did you do that?"

She looked at him and smiled, "Maths is just a game, enjoy it! Everything will be easy! You can win over it!"

2007

FORTY-FOUR

Omkar now had moved to the ninth grade. Kiran had moved to the seventh.

Omkar gets sexually attracted towards other girls and starts ignoring Kiran. Whereas, ignorance makes Kiran became more possessive about him. Earlier they used to spend as much as possible time with each other in the school.

Kiran was with his behaviour and was unable to understand why was he behaving so different!

The recess bell rang. The students ran out of their classrooms. It was a strict order by the Principal, 'to have food outside the classroom, expect during rainy season and only if a lecture is extended and overlaps the break partially.'

This overlap usually happened between ninth and tenth standard for some specific lectures!

Many children had brought their individual lunch box. Yet some of them had come empty handed; they bought food stuffs from the canteen and poor children were given food items provided by the government.

Omkar and his group usually have their lunch in their classroom. They didn't care for about principal's notice. He was accompanied by four of his friends and two girls. They all belong to the same class and division.

Well you would know how arrogant children become when they reach ninth! You may have a similar experience!

The dark clouds have covered the school. The wind is carrying a cool breeze. The climate is cool and romantic.

Kiran moved out of her class. She walked to Omkar's class. Kiran murmured, "I will keep an eye on him!"

She reached his classroom. She walked in. Everyone was busy having food. Almost every other girl had a boyfriend. She glanced at Omkar. Omkar was sitting on the third bench of the last row from the entrance with his group, four boys and two girls, one of whom was Sofia. Sofia was sitting next to Omkar. His friends were sitting on the front table.

Sofia was Omkar's classmate. She was fair and beautiful with long hair. She was Omkar's girl-friend!

Unnoticed Kiran walked in the first row. She went to the last bench. She slowly moved to the last row. She quietly went towards the three benches ahead. She sat and put her hands on the bench and folded them. She glanced at Omkar. She murmured "I don't want to lose you Omkar!"

She sat with her head in her hands. She covered her face. She peeped through the gaps of her fingers. Sofia got up. She said, "I will be back, let me wash my hands."

She walked out of the classroom. Omkar looked at her with lust in his eyes. Kiran's eyes grew bigger! They admired her curves. Omkar said "I have opened a facebook account! Guys you can add me!"

The class replied, "Fine!

Omkar bit his tongue and murmured "Oops! I was so loud!"

Vishal commented, "She is looking hot today!"

Omkar gave him an angry look. He replied, "Doesn't she?"

Omkar replied, "Yes!" He gave a fight to Omkar.

Ajinkya replied, "I have heard that this is the age where we all are in love with all the girls around us!"

Omkar commented, "Everyone looks hot and sexy!""

They laughed. They gave a group fight. They happily said, "Science teacher also said that we are growing children!"

Omkar replied, "But now I am confused!"

His friend inquired, "About what?"

He shared, "Do I love Sofia? And is this correct?"

Sanjay answered, "Well unless you try how you will come to know is it correct! So enjoy each and every moment!"

Omkar inquired, "Stop it man! You were supposed to bring a magazine of hot women in bikinis!"

Sanjay replied, "I have got it!"

He got up. He went to his place. He opened the zip of his bag and removed a magazine. He closed his bag. He came back to them. He sat next to Omkar. He opened it. Everyone looked at the magazine from back to front.

"Wow!" Omkar reacted. Kiran stretched her neck up. Omkar commented, "She is hot!"

Vishal said, "She is in a two piece!"

He pointed at her clothes.

Ajinkya commented, "Beautiful!"

Omkar said, "She is hot!"

Sanjay said, "But I am not happy!"

Everyone looked at him strangely. He continued, "She should have been bare-bodied!"

Omkar commented, "Wow!"

Vishal noticed Sofia coming back. He turned emotionless. The lust disappeared from his face. He turned red. He quickly pulled the magazine and kept it in the shelf. They looked at her. Sofia looked at them. Everyone was red faced. She questioned, "What happened? Why have you all become red?"

"No! No!! Nothing!"

"Are you sure?"

"Yes!" replied Omkar. He looked in her eyes. He dipped into her eyes.

Vishal and others replied, "Yes of course!"

The bell rang. Omkar stammered, "Break, break is over!"

Omkar again checked her curves. Sofia said, "Back to your places friends!"

The students rushed back to their respective classes. The school became empty. Kiran escaped in the crowd. She remained unnoticed. The space was filled with students.

Sofia sat next to Omkar. He kept her hand on her back. She looked at him. He looked at her. He couldn't imagine what would be her reaction. He moved his palm on her back. She smiled.

The class-teacher came in.

A student reacted, "It's not her period! Why is she here?"

Everyone got up. Everyone wished her, "Good afternoon mam!"

She replied "Good afternoon! Boys form a line outside the classroom! You need to go to the auditorium! There is a program for you people!"

A boy questioned, "And what about girls?"

She replied, "They will have the program here itself!"

Omkar whispered in his group, "I know what the program is all about!"

Vishal inquired, "What is it about?"

He replied "Sex!"

Sofia giggled. She covered her mouth with her hands. The boys got up and moved out.

FORTY-FIVE

Two Ways

One evening, it happened to be Sunday! Due to some emergency case, Dr. Pooja had to go to the hospital immediately; Ajinkya had gone out due to some work! And Kiran was left all alone in the house! It's well said, an idle mind is Devil's workshop!

The Devil began his act! She went and stood in front of the dressing table. She stripped-off. She looked at her reflection and cursed, "Why can't I be like Sofia? Why?"

She threw her comb down; she sat on the floor and looked down. Her anger flashed from her eyes. As time passed by she calmed herself.

She called Omkar's home phone number. Luckily, Omkar answered the phone, "Hello!"

Kiran inquired "Hi! Omkar?"

"Yes!" he replied.

"Kiran! Listen na! I am alone! I am scared! Please come home na!" she pleaded.

He thought for some time and replied "Fine! I am coming!"

Kiran pleaded again "And please don't carry books!"

"Fine!" he said and kept the receiver.

In next fifteen minutes, Omkar was outside her house. He knocked the door. She looked through the magic eye. Her eyes grew big. She removed the guarder from her long shiny black silky hair and kept it open to the front. She opened the door. He stepped in.

She had worn a mini-skirt and a shiny white shirt with sleeves folded till the elbow. He scanned her. The top button was left open.

She locked the door. She said, "Let's sit in the bedroom!"

"Fine!" Omkar replied with a gradually bold voice. The Adam's apple jumped up.

He washed his feet and then he went in the bedroom. He sat on the bed at a distance from Kiran.

Omkar looked at her. He scanned her thoroughly this time. He approached her slowly. And He stopped right in front of her.

The Desperate Devil quickly got transferred into Omkar like a viral virus! He overshadowed Omkar's conscience.

The Good declared a war against The Devil. He required Omkar's contribution and support to win. But Omkar betrayed!

Omkar signed a treaty of physical training and The Devil declared his victory! He pushed Omkar towards the valley of lust. Omkar fell from the valley of lust. And soon The Good shrieked.

"C'mon get over her!"

The Devil commanded and began his physical training. Omkar walked towards her with heavy legs.

"Yes! That's it!" The Devil responded.

She closed her eyes. She accepted Omkar's dictatorship.

"The girl is serving herself in front of you! Have her and she will not tell anyone about it! C'mon! Yes you can!"

Omkar remained numb. He walked ahead. A cold drop of sweat ran down his neck. He approached with thirsty lips.

She felt his warmth. She raised her thirsty lips to him. He gripped her firmly in his arms. He kissed her neck. She closed her eyes. He kissed her lips. He drove his warm palm on her bare back.

He interlocked her. He navigated the world! She opened her eyes. Omkar looked in her eyes.

Omkar slipped through her beautiful eyes. He traveled to the her heart with a lightened speed. Kiran was always an open book for Omkar. He saw his pic hanged with love, trust and faith on the wall of her heart!

That pic challenged his love and washed off the power of the Devil! Slowly and gradually The Good became powerful.

His soul challenged his heart, "What are you doing?"

He lost the command over her. His firm interlocked arms parted.

The Good commanded,

"She loves you! She trusts you! And you are breaking her trust! You are confused! You are in a relation with Sofia! Don't forget that!"

He pulled his hand back. The Good explained, "What about her? Do you love Sofia?"

A line of stress appeared on his forehead.

"You love Sofia right? So what are you doing?"

He pushed himself back. She looked in his eyes. A drop of tear came out of her eyes.

Omkar could hear echoes - Sofia, Sofia, Sofia, Kiran, Kiran, Kiran! Sofia, Kiran, Sofia (and after a pause) Kiran!

"What's wrong?" Kiran cooed.

He went numb and a thought flashed in his mind. A minute later, he took a deep breath and said to Kiran "See! I...I...I love you!" He took a pause.

His heart started pumping more blood. He recited, "See I LOVE YOU. But this is NOT RIGHT!"

She looked at his face.

"If I love, I love you and this is not right!"

He started stammering, "I? I mean! I love you! This! This is not right!"

She looked at his shivering lips.

"I don't know what exactly I want to say? I don't know how to express it!"

He wiped the sweat from his forehead.

"See I need sometime! If, if I love? I love you then? THEN I will come back to you! But right now I am confused!"

He said in a calm voice, "Trust, TRUST ME! I need some time!"

He walked away. He looked at her. He turned back. He walked out of the room. She gazed at him.

He walked out and this gave rise to numerous different questions in her mind.

She questioned with herself. "So did he mean that he loves me? What was he trying to say?"

She turned back and sat on the bed.

"Will he come back?

Have I lost my love?

Have I lost my good friend?"

These questions piled up in the store room of her brain. They remained unanswered.

Omkar started avoiding Sofia. Their relationship went through dark patch. And Sofia decided to move ahead with different guy of another division. Omkar behaved like a stranger, as if he never knew Sofia. But he didn't come back to Kiran.

This gap increased day by day and it became a huge big wall! Her questions remained unanswered. And these questions took away her peace and happiness.

Omkar prioritized his studies. For him studies became very important and not a girl! He wanted to have a girl friend since childhood, but as time passed, he learnt that a girl is not everything! His work can make a difference in his life! Rahul had moved out of the house. Now he needs to live like a responsible kid!

FORTY-SIX

Two weeks had passed by. Kiran had become absent minded. Pooja noticed the silence.

Kiran now was teenager.

At this age a kid goes through hormonal changes. They start growing physical. She required proper support and guidance. At this age everyone tend to commit mistakes. So they need additional care! Pooja realized this! She decided to start an investigation.

Pooja tried to analyze Kiran by her sweet talks. But Kiran didn't reveal anything. Kiran spent a good time with Pooja. At times, in the middle of the talks, Kiran gained the famous silence. Kiran was lost in her own world!

Many a times Kiran left her talks incomplete! But Pooja understood the emotions behind them.

Pooja concluded her investigation.

Kiran needs consultation!

Confidence, eternal peace and focus had washed off!

Kiran needs help!!

One Sunday evening, Ajinkya was busy watching dance show on television. He was sitting on the couch wearing a white plain T-shirt and a skin colour three-fourth.

Pooja came and sat next to him. She whispered, "Ajinkya, you need to speak with Kiran"

He looked at Pooja. Pooja continued "Something is wrong with her! She is quiet and sad. I tried to speak, but she did not share with me! She tried to hide it by giving a fake smile!"

Ajinkya switched off the television by the red button of the remote. He thought for a while. And then he got up. He went in the bedroom. The lights were switched off. The room looked like a dark cave! Kiran was sitting alone. He switched on the lights; but she was still in her own world! He sat next to her. He tapped her shoulder.

She looked at Ajinkya. She was shocked to see him. She tried to give him a forcible smile but she failed!

She said, “Hi Dad!”

He replied, “Where were you lost?”

She instantly replied back, “No where!”

Pooja came at the door and halted. Ajinkya replied in a serious voice, “Stop lying! Your face is telling me something else!”

Kiran hugged Ajinkya. She locked him tight with his arms. She busted into tears. Suddenly a cracker exploded. Ajinkya inquired, “Hey what happen?” and tapped her back.

Kiran said, “I am sorry!”

Ajinkya remained numb. She calmed. Ajinkya questioned, “Hey what happen dear? Why are you crying? Did Omkar do anything?”

She denied by nodding her head. She continued, “But I am feeling lonely! I am feeling as if, something is wrong with me! First my parents left me; later life brought me to different workplaces, where everyone used me! I want love, but everyone is behind money! I am about to lose my love!”

She wept again. Ajinkya inquired, “Great you’re in love!”

Kiran didn't reply. But rather she became quiet. Ajinkya continued, "What happened?" He tapped her shoulder and said, "Stop crying first! Tell what happened?"

He wiped her eyes and left. He went to the terrace of his building. He gave a ring on Omkar's landline.

Tring! Tring!! Omkar's mother answered the call, "Hello!"

He replied, "Hello Aunty, Is Omkar there?"

"Yes! He is busy watching Indian Idol!"

He replied, "I have some work! Send him to the terrace!"

She replied "Sure! I will send him right now! But is there any problem?"

He consoled, "No! Nothing serious!"

She kept the receiver and looked at Omkar. She said, "Omkar Ajinkya is calling you to his terrace!"

She went in the kitchen. Omkar got up. He was wearing a maroon sleeveless T-shirt and a maroon night-pant. He wore his sandals and left. His mother came in the hall. She picked the remote and switched off the television and went in.

FORTY-SEVEN

Omkar climbed the stairs to the terrace. He looked at Ajinkya. Ajinkya was busy on a call. He wrapped the call. He walked to Omkar. He kept his arms on Omkar's shoulder.

He started, "How are you?"

With a tense face Omkar replied, "I am fine!"

He inquired, "Are you in love?"

He instantly replied back, "No!"

Ajinkya looked at him. He said, "So what happened between you and Kiran?"

He looked down. He ran his eyes up at Ajinkya and again looked down. He narrated the whole story. Ajinkya hugged him.

Ajinkya consoled him, "Om, don't worry! Everything will be fine! It happens at this age! I will take care of this! Take care of yourself! Live your life, think much! Or else life will turn into disaster! I will speak with Kiran!"

They sat on the down on the terrace. Ajinkya held Omkar tight in his arms and said, "Remember I am always there with your! You're the best! Trust me you can overcome this! You know what those stars high up in the sky will give you power to fight

He maintained silence for few minutes looked up to the sky! The world seemed to be beautiful. The scenary around them was amazing, as the sun rested to the west! The yellowish sky and the cold current gave peace to them!

Ajinkya held Omkar's hand and looked in his eyes. He said do you know at his age everyone has went through this face, may it be me, your bro, or your dad! It happens to all! But it's normal! Life is beautiful and sex is not the thing in life! You have got an opportunity to live a good life! Live it properly and make a difference!"

He looked at the nature around. The darkness spread all around and the street lights and the headlights of the vehicles flashed around. The stars were in the sky as well as on the land!

Ajinkya said, Om relax! Take time! You can take your time! You have a right to get confused! Just one thing, don't we are there with you always!

He held Omkar firm in his arms.

FORTY-EIGHT

Ajinkya walked down; Omkar went back to his home. Ajinkya went to Pooja. He murmured something in her ears. She sat on the couch for a while. Kiran was in the bedroom still weeping. She went in the bedroom.

She sat next to Kiran. She held her arms. Kiran looked down. She picked her face. She looked into her eyes. She said in a calm voice, "Kiran! Forget what happened in the past, live in the present and your future will be good! Think about this! In this age guys blabber their naughty talks! If a girl lets a guy over shadow her persona, usually boys have fun and leave her! But Om did not do that because, he knew that he might misuse your faith! And by this he might lose your trust! Maybe he did not want to hurt you! But right now, think about this! First you lost your family, but now you have a family. You worked hard to go back to school, you are back there! So why are you thinking negative?"

Ajinkya stepped in. Pooja continued, "I am there, your mom! AJ, your dad is with you! We love you!"

Ajinkya inquired, "Was he your first love?"

She denied by nodding her head sideways. A drop of water fell from Pooja's eyes. Ajinkya asked, "Then who is your first love?"

She pointed her finger at Ajinkya. Ajinkya was shocked and remained numb. He looked at her sparkling eyes. A second later, he replied, "Then love me! I am still yours!" Kiran looked at him. She got up and wiped her eyes. She ran towards Ajinkya and hugged him. She said, "AJ I love you!"

Ajinkya held her firm in her arms and replied I love you too dear!

She kept her head on his shoulder. She said, dad what is Facebook?

It's a social networking site where you can connect with your friends, neighbours! Why?

She replied I want to open a facebook account! Can you help me dad?

Ajinkya rubbed her back and looked at Pooja. Pooja gave an affirmative sign by her eyes. And then he replied, "Fine! I will open an account for you! Don't worry!" I too need to open an account there!

He kissed her cheeks. Pooja wiped her eyes. Kiran kissed Ajinkya's lips.

Back to 2015

FORTY-NINE

I heard someone calling, RJ Kiran, RJ Kiran! And I enjoyed the call! But suddenly I realized I was sleeping. I opened my eyes. Instantaneously, the characters, one by one, disappeared from my sight. And I was pushed back to the present! I looked at the door. My manager peeped through the door. I replied, "Yes sir!"

The Manager opened the door. He said, "Well Sameer will be late you take over the show!"

I questioned with shock, "Are you sure?"

He added "Yes RJ Kiran, but only for the next thirty minutes!"

"That's wonderful! " she replied.

The Manager took me to the RJ room. I opened the door. The room was empty. I looked at the Manager. He replied, "Best of luck!"

I nodded my head with confidence. I went in and sat on the chair. I looked at the equipments and screens there. I said, "I can't believe I will be on air today!"

I closed my eyes. I closed my fist and took a deep breath. Suddenly the radio phone rang. "I am live on air, now!" I exaggerated.

I answered the phone, "Hello!"

"Hello RJ?" the person at the other end replied.

I replied, "Yes! Who is it?"

He answered "I am Ravi from Nigdi!"

I asked, "How are you?"

"I am fine! I just wrapped up tea at a tea stall and I dialed your number. I am lucky that the call didn't hit the waiting-list!"

"Hmm!"

I inquired "So did you find chotu working there?"

He commented "Oh yes that late current chotu! But how do you know him? Do you live around?"

I smiled and then replied, "No I don't! That's sad that still in this city people allow and practice child labour!"

"Oh that's fine!" he replied after laughing. "That actually is a symbol of being in India! It's Poor India!"

He laughed again. This comment hammered my sense of pride.

I replied, "Well let me educate you about something!"

He replied, "Ah?"

"My country is the richest country in the world in terms of man-power! The most intelligent people are from India. If everyone works in a proper manner, you will not see any chotu working anywhere! Have you ever inquired why is he working? Every child wants to enjoy his/her life and some children also love to study. Maximum love to play! Then why are they working?"

He commented "Why should I?"

I took a deep breath and I replied.

This is the symbol poor human being! This world only understands the sound of money. Here we don't respect living beings, and that's where we are wrong! Everything here works hand-in-hand! We should actually give our best to earn money and educate our children. But everyone doesn't do that! That's the reason why a small child has to become mentally strong. He has work hard and earns his bread and butter. For this, either he loses his education or else works during the day and goes to the night school! In this city, it still happens! Every father desires a boy! Don't you?"

I took a sigh. I took a deep breath which boosted confidence! The back end member of the radio station selected the song 'Vande Mataram' on the media player. He kept the volume of microphone on a higher pace and music at the soft level. The person at the other end kept quiet.

Vance mataram vande mataram...

I continued "But still we say, we are Educated! Well let me tell you one more thing. The 2nd richest person in the world today had failed in exams and our top cricketer Sachin Tendulkar has as well! Education enhances our thinking. But what we have to do will Prove Our Intelligence! Anyway I think it doesn't matter to you, right! No country is poor or rich, good or bad! Its people living there, that are good or bad, and their thinking!"

The person at the other end hung up.

But I continued, "My name is Kiran. I too was a child labourer. But Ajinkya took my responsibility so today I am here speaking with you!

I acquired a deep listen and then I continued,

I am lucky that I am not a part of that thing anymore! And He is my first love! Radio Rocks! I Love My India! This country has given us everything then why do we abuse her! We need to join our hands change the life of those who say 'I Hate My Life!'"

I took my overwhelming emotions. I stopped with a pride on my face! The employees of radio rocks stood up. The whole staff gave me a standing applause. The children working at different places are listening to the Radio. They might have liked it!

I rested my back on the chair. Then I realized that the man had already disconnected the line. I looked at the computer screen. Slowly appreciation messages flooded the inbox. People became crazy and they started sending messages on the Radio Rocks number.

Suddenly I heard a knock at the door. I looked back. I saw my manager peeping in through the semi-transparent glass. I walked to the door and opened it. Manager greeted me with a smile.

He said, "I heard your talk. You sound good! We were actually working on a new show coming next month. In that show, people can call in and tell their problems and RJ will give them advice and probe them to become a good human being. The channel has signed deals with some brands for the show!"

He paused. I eagerly glanced at him.

"I will introduce you in that show! But for the timing, you'll work under other RJs. And that will help you to know how theory is different, than practical work!"

I was overwhelmed when he shook hands with me.

He replied, "You're done for today! Come tomorrow the same time."

I was unable to control blushing. I moved out of the cabin. Everyone in the office greeted me for the way she answered. RJ Reshma walked to me.

RJ Reshma said, "You have a very good and lovely voice! It's just that I felt you were aggressive on the phone!"

She sounded annoyed with my talk. And I replied, "I love my country! " and she walked away. RJ Reshma looked back and stared at her confidence and spark.

RJ Reshma walked to the manager. Manager said, "You go ahead and take over the show, RJ Reshma!"

She kept quiet and went in. I halted at the reception. I collected my I-phone. Suddenly my cell phone vibrated.

It said - '1 New Message'

There are two options right below it. 'View' and 'Exit'. I eagerly opened the message.

I murmured, "I hope, it's Omkar!"

It said,

I'm back from States.
The tour was excllnt and it ll help the company expnd.
Meet you in sumtym.
Regards,
AJ.
President - Overseas
Bill track India Pvt. Ltd

A smile unknowingly appeared on my face.

A Month later today I am going to meet Ajinkya! " I murmured.

FIFTY

Mumbai International Airport.

Ajinkya and Mr. Chaubey along wih their research team stepped out from Terminus 2.

They took the company cab and within two hours they were at the outskirts of Pune.

Everyone was tired and deep asleep. The only three people were awake, the driver, Mr. Chaubey and Ajinkya. Mr. Chaubey was busy reviewing a mail received from United States Business Head. And Ajinkya was busy trying Pooja's cell phone. Her cell phone rang couple of times but she seemed to be busy. She didn't answer the call!

He tried once again. And this time she answered the phone instantly.

"Pooja were you busy?'

"I just woke up!"

Ajinkya inquired, "Why so late?"

"Yesterday I was in the hospital the entire night! There was an emergency!"

"Ok! How is Kiran?"

"Don't know! She is not in the house! Please try her cell!"

"Ok!"

Ajinkya disconnected the phone.

Ajinkya started thinking about something. Suddenly he heard a known voice. He looked around. He found that, he and a cab driver were the only people traveling in the cab. He asked himself, "Is my cell phone ringing?"

He checked it, "No its not! But I have heard this voice somewhere! The voice is barely audible!"

Ajinkya inquired, "Bhaiya, are you playing some music?"

He replied, "No! It's the radio! Should I turn it off?"

"No! Increase the volume!"

The driver increased the volume. Ajinkya reacted to himself, "Hey this is Kiran! How is she on air?"

He inquired "Which channel is it?"

"It's Radio Rocks!" he replied.

Soon he reached his new residence.

FIFTY-ONE

Tring! Tring! Ajinkya's cell phone rang. Tring! Tring! He got down from the cab. He answered the phone, "Hello!"

The person on the other side said, "Hi! Ajinkya bhaiya I am coming home!"

"Hey! How are you Omkar? " From the other end.

"I am fine! " Ajinkya replied, "So when are you reaching here?"

"In fifteen minutes! " Omkar replied.

C'mon! Come fast! I am waiting for you! " said Ajinkya and he disconnected the call. A smile appeared on his tired face.

“He has been in Mumbai for four years now to complete his degree in animation from a top international university, Ajinkya murmured. I will see him after long time!

The cab went back to the office. He climbed the stairs of his bungalow. He rang the door-bell. Pooja opened the door. He went in. She took his travel bag from his hand. He dragged the suitcase in the bedroom.

She inquired with a smile, “How was your journey?”

“Good! ” Ajinkya replied.

She kept the bag on the couch. She went in the kitchen and came with a glass of water.

“Uff! I am tired!”

“Yes I know! ” She answered and gave the glass. He took a sip.

“But I can see a different smile on your face? ” she inquired.

“Yes! Omkar is coming in fifteen minutes! ” He replied.

“That’s great!”

“We all would have lunch together this afternoon! ” he commented.

Ajinkya called, "Omkar where are you? I am waiting for you!"

He replied, "AJ, I have some important work. I will be there asap! Please hold the line"

And Omkar placed his call on hold.

I am Kiran! I walked out of Radio Rocks building with a smile on my face. Everyone liked my voice. I had impressed my boss. My dream job is secured. I said.

I preferred to walk, rather to take a rickshaw during this hot sunny day. Suddenly my cell phone vibrated. I halted near a bus stop and looked at the cell phone. It displayed '1 New message'

I selected 'view'. I murmured with a surprise "From Omkar! Today I received his first message since he has taken my cell number four years back!"

The message said 'I want 2 meet u n speak with u now! I m in Pune!'

A guy standing next to her said, "Hey did you hear to that new RJ on Radio Rocks?"

The other guy replied "Yeah! Her name is RJ Kiran!"

He expressed, “Her voice is so sweet!”

The other guy replied, “It would be better if she does early morning show! She would make everyone’s day with her sweet voice! Hey let’s search on Fb!”

Hearing to this I blushed with joy. Suddenly my cell phone vibrated again. Omkar inquired,’whr r u??’

I replied, ‘near S.T. Bus stop swargate’

He replied, ‘f9 lets meet @ hotel aura’

I texted, ‘k’

It’s for the first time we were messaging each other. I walked to Hotel Aura. I was desperate to know why Omkar wants to meet her. I murmured, “Suddenly why does he want to meet me? What does he want speak?”

I walked in. I sat at table number one near the entrance. There was a round table covered with white cloth. Two chairs facing each other.

RJ Reshma updated about the pleasant weather on the low volume digital radio transistor.

Suddenly the studio phone ranged. RJ Reshma answered the call, “Radio Rocks?”

She replied, “Yes! Who’s this?”

"Hi my name is Omkar Kale! Actually I love someone and want to propose her on air!"

"That's great!" she replied, "So what's her name?"

"Her name is Kiran Kulkarni!" he replied.

RJ Reshma recollected about RJ Kiran and her face flashed in RJ Reshma's mind.

He continued, "Well I have her dad means my best friend AJ on a three way call right now!"

She said, "Great! So what are you waiting for?"

I looked around. A couple was sitting at my right. The guy whispered may be some romantic lines and she blushed. I looked at the door and rolled my silky shiny long hair on my ring finger. I comprehended, "So what does he want to speak with me?"

I blinked my eyes. I rubbed my feet with each other. I murmured, "So when is he coming?"

I looked at the door. And suddenly a good physique guy walked in. He asked the manager sitting at reception to increase the volume. He walked to me like a hero does in melodrama. He reminded her entry of Shah Rukh Khan in Kabhi Khushi Kabhie Gaam. I glanced at his physique which appeared through his red T-shirt and black jeans pant, black leather jacket over it and a fastrack goggle and fastrack watch on his left wrist. He also had a Bluetooth on his right ear. He removed his goggle and kept it in the pocket of his jacket.

He sat quite in front of me at the same table.

I glanced at him again. He sat quite. I looked my wrist watch and then looked at the door. He stared me. I looked at him again with anger.

I smiled. I rested my elbows on the table. He said with hesitation, "Hi!"

Omkar explained, "I think you did not recognize me! Hi, I am Omkar!"

I replied with a shocking expression on my face, "Huh!"

I stared at him. Years had passed, we hadn't heard anything from each other. And it seemed very difficult to begin the conversation.

Almost fifteen minutes later, Omkar said, "H...How is you?"

I replied, "I...I am fine! How are you?"

Omkar replied, "I am fine!"

I inquired, "How come you are in Pune? When did you come?"

He took a deep breath. He replied, “I just arrived!”

I inquired again, “On bike?”

He smiled and replied, “Yeah!”

Few seconds later, he asked, “What would you like to have?”

I crushed her eagerness by locking my hand tight in my left palm. I replied, “No. Ma is waiting for me! I can’t wait any longer! You wanted to speak with me?”

RJ Reshma murmured, “For sure she is RJ Kiran! This is her voice!”

He replied, “Yes! Uh..!”

He looked to his right and inquired, “So do you love Prashant?”

I answered in passive voice, “Hmm! Why? What happen?”

He replied, “No. No. Nothing!”

He murmured, “Omkar say you love me!”

Ajinkya prompted, “You idiot, come directly to the point Omkar!”

RJ Reshma said, “Yes, c’mon!”

I commented, "Who is this RJ shouting? What's going on the radio?"

RJ Reshma became numb. Omkar looked around. I inquired, "So are you done?" And I started leaving. He raised his right hand pointing towards me and he eagerly said, "Wait!"

I looked his numb face and sat back at my place. He inquired again, "Do you love Prashant?"

I became aggressive and started rolling the end of my dupatta on my right finger below. I questioned him back, "What do you want to ask? Come to the point! I am getting late!"

He took a deep breath to overcome his fast running heartbeats. And I looked at him and murmured, "C'mon say it! I am losing my patience! I can't wait any longer!"

He looked in my eyes. We established an eye contact!

He collected words from the different corners of his brains. He took a deep breath again. He said, "You are quite! It means you don't love him!"

I looked in his eyes. He said, "That means I am not late!"

I murmured, "Why does he not come direct to the point?"

He continued with hesitating voice, "I.. I love you Kiran!"

He went down on his knees. He questioned in his strong confident voice, "Will you become my life partner?"

The crowd around stood to see what's going on. Ajinkya nibbled his nails. I looked at him with my happy sparkling eyes so remove his fear. I gave my hand in his hand and said, "Yes!"

Now I placed the ball in his court! He stood up. He blushed and looked at me. RJ Reshma said, "Congratulations Omkar and Kiran!"

I looked up at him. He disconnected and said, "Right now, we were live on Radio Rocks!"

Omkar hugged me.

RJ Reshma announced, "This song goes for this couple. May they have a happy life! And people stay tuned Punekars, a while layer we will have Rahul Kale the blockbuster writer, with us on this show! So stay tuned!"

They left the hotel hand-in-hand. He drove his red sports bike. I rested on the back seat. He was happy. But I was stressed.

I whispered, "You are too much! You gave me a shock again!" And I smiled.

"Oh!" He blushed remembering his childishness.

He whispered, "Yes I have made MISTAKES; BECAUSE MY LIFE did not come with An INSTRUCTION MANUAL!"

He whispered, "I love you!"

I whispered, "I love you too!"

He whispered, "You are stunning and sexy since childhood. It's just I was confused and I required some time!"

I replied, "Almost seven to eight years!"

He replied, "Yes, I mean to say no! But you know what I was the first to know about your secret!"

I smiled and gripped his back with my arms.

FIFTY-TWO

It's six in the evening. The weather was pleasant outside. The sun had turned yellowish at the west; there were different shades which décor the sky with white clouds and a thin film like moon. A cold breeze is running down the street.

I sat on the couch with a cup of tea in my hand. All the others were sitting in the balcony enjoying the scenario. I picked Ajinkya's laptop and switched it on. I logged onto facebook.

There all most thirty messages and many different notifications posted on my account. All most everyone had congratulated me for today. My breast grew with confidence. I updated, "Today, I feel like I am a celebrity! Thank you my friends!"

I rested my back and I recollected the whole day. I looked at my facebook account and refreshed again! Prashant commented, "Proud of you!"

I just ignored it. I posted one more update, Good news!! Good news!! Soon I am getting engaged with Omkar!

Prashant stared my update and couldn't react. He jumped into my profile. He selected unfriend. It questioned, 'Are you sure you want unfriend?'

He said 'Yes!'

The End